# I Still Love Him

Tracy-Ann Lewis

iUniverse, Inc.
Bloomington

# I Still Love Him

*Copyright © 2010 by Tracy-Ann Lewis*
*All rights reserved. No part of this book may be used or reproduced*
*by any means, graphic, electronic, or mechanical, including*
*photocopying, recording, taping or by any information storage*
*retrieval system without the written permission of the publisher*
*except in the case of brief quotations embodied in critical articles and*
*reviews.*

*This is a work of fiction. All of the characters, names, incidents,*
*organizations, and dialogue in this novel are either the products*
*of the author's imagination or are used fictitiously.*

*iUniverse books may be ordered through booksellers or by contacting:*

*iUniverse*
*1663 Liberty Drive*
*Bloomington, IN 47403*
*www.iuniverse.com*
*1-800-Authors (1-800-288-4677)*

*Because of the dynamic nature of the Internet, any Web addresses or*
*links contained in this book may have changed since publication and*
*may no longer be valid. The views expressed in this work are solely*
*those of the author and do not necessarily reflect the views of the*
*publisher, and the publisher hereby disclaims any responsibility for*
*them.*

*ISBN: 978-1-4502-5442-7 (sc)*
*ISBN: 978-1-4502-5443-4 (ebook)*

*Printed in the United States of America*

*iUniverse rev. date: 11/16/2010*

I was born and raised in the country part of Jamaica, in the parish of St. Elizabeth, real fucking country! Cannot and will not get any more country than that. If you are invited for dinner in St. Elizabeth make sure that you do not eat for a day before you go, because they serve some big ass yams, about six to seven dumplings, and a chicken that is as big as a turkey on Thanksgiving Day. But I love the country, it was all I knew, so I never thought for one second that I would be living in one of the biggest mansion in Harbor View, Kingston, and married to one of the wealthiest man. Until one day when I met Charles Anderson, at the time he was the owner of some of the biggest car dealerships in Jamaica and a Counselor at the University, at a restaurant on my lunch break across from the University of the West Indies. I was about three months pregnant with my daughter Lacy. Charles and I immediately liked each other. Even when I informed him I was pregnant he still insisted on us getting married, right away, and I agreed, and still couldn't find the answer to the question why?

With all the money and respect that I got from just presenting myself as Mrs. Anderson still couldn't stop me from feeling lonely every time Charles would call and said he was working late. Most of the time he don't even bother calling at all. He had me thinking about my first love and spent nights of wondering where he was and whose arms he was sleeping in. I asked God to let him forgive me for walking out on him and marrying to someone else without giving him a chance to fix what I believed was a problem.

# Chapter One
# How it all begins?

On Careen's seventeenth birthday, June 28, 2000, she decided to go out and celebrate with her two best friends. It was not only her birthday but also their high school graduation weekend and she insisted that Club H would be the best place for them that night.

She was very happy when her grandparents agreed that she could go, she is now seventeen. But still didn't feel right about leaving without asking, and knowing mama Tee, she didn't care what age you were, she still felt you had to show respect at all times even if you were no longer living under her roof. Careen didn't have no need to remember those rules because loving and respecting her grandparents was something that she was born with so it always came out naturally. They took her in and cared for her when her parents died two years earlier in a car accident. Their love and support were some of the reasons she found her strength to move on.

Right after the conversation with Mama Tee she went to her room and started getting dressed in a fitted black slick dress that her friend Destiny had brought back for her birthday gift on her trip from Miami two days ago. The dress was hot and so was Careen she had the most beautiful long legs and the shape of a Coke bottle her, smooth dark skin was as soft as her silk dress and a pair of brown eyes that would make any man fall in love. Her body was firm from walking up and down those hills back and Forth to school every day. She looked real good and she knew it. She couldn't walk down the street without someone calling after her. Men of all ages did it and in all different types of situations young and old, men on foot, in cars, even men on donkeys... some fucking nerve. Careen knew their intentions, all they wanted was to turn her in all sorts of positions and she wasn't falling for it - her virginity was her treasure one that she was planning on keeping for Mr. Right.

"Careen, let's go. My cousin Steve is going to give us a ride."

"I'm coming Kerry-Ann I just need to find shoes to go with this dress."

"Here you go, sis, my birthday gift to you."

Careen slightly lift her head from looking under the bed to the hottest silver and black sandals she had ever seen in any store. "

I saw the dress Destiny brought for you and I figure you could use this shoes to go with it."

"Thanks Kerry-Ann have I ever told you that you are my girl for life?"

"Yes you did but only when I give you something."

They both laughed, on their way to the car Careen ask Kerry-Ann if she called Destiny to remind her to meet them at the club.

"Yes I did but I'm not sure if she is coming."

"Why you say that? It is my birthday celebration. She'd never miss out on that."

"True that, but she sound like she was having some wild sex, but don't worry Careen she will come."

"She better and her ass better not be late either."

"I have to give it up to you though, sis your hair looks good. I'm so please that you decided to let your auntie glue some extensions instead of catching it up into a ponytail and gelling down the sides with bangs at the front. All you needed was a lunch kit and you could be back in basic school again."

"Fuck off Kerry-Ann."

By then they were both dying with laughter, trying to catch their breath for the next word.

"For real though it look nice, and please act your age tonight and not like when you were twelve at my birthday party when you wanted to go home to mommy because the music was too grown up for you. You are beautiful and sexy, so hold your head up and stop walking around with that shy ass attitude because that is not working for the man this year," Kerry-Ann said as she brushed her hair from her face.

Careen was enjoying the drive looking outside the window thinking about a career choice she could care less about what her girl had to say, she was always a leader and only does what she wanted because her mother once told her the choices she made today would be the ones that affected her tomorrow.

"Look Careen I'm sorry for mentioning your mom" Kerry-Ann said sadly.

"It's ok sis."

"I know you had never been to clubs before but act as if you had been there a thousand times. You are the queen of it tonight - you have the dress and the body to go with it so work it like you're proud."

"Ok Kerry-Ann you always want to be my instructor and school me on these shit. I don't know who give you that title but go ahead and use it, because I am who I am and I am not changing don't matter how much you teach. Not that I am shy but I talk to whom I want when I want. So please stay out of

3

my life." She kissed her teeth and turned her attention back to looking out the window. "That is not going to happen we been through basic school, primary school and high school together and you best believe my ass is right, besides you arms in arms at the university of the west Indies."

"If you say so, we should have thought about going to different colleges."

"Why would you want to do a fool thing like that? We are getting married together as well."

"Watch your words Kerry-Ann."

"You know what I mean because I don't play that."

"If you say so. Talking about marriage, when are we going to meet this Dwayne that you been dating for two years now. How come you never let us see him?"

"No specific reason. Remember he lives in May Pen and most of the time he goes to Miami to help his father with his hardware store. So the little time we spend together I don't want you and Destiny there. We spend a lot of time talking on the phone and I enjoy it."

"Well whatever work for you if you are happy then I am happy for you, I'm sure we will meet him sometime soon."

"You will meet him soon, he been back about a week ago he wanted to come and look for me but he said he have some business to take care of so I tell him not to stress it. Whenever he finds the time he can come."

"Ok, whatever you say just make sure you and Destiny don't even think about leaving me sitting here by myself to go broke out on the dance floor,"

Careen said.

"I love you sis, but I cannot promise you that. What if a song comes on 'bout if a gal a sleep with mi man mi can't sit down mi have to go bounce a gal to"

"You better cut that out before you get into a fight because mi look too good for that tonight."

"No need for that. I have no competition out there and

the few who act like they want to try and match up to me - I already beat them asses."

"Kerry-Ann please how could somebody want your man when no one knows him?" "Whatever Careen, Dwayne has already proven to me that his heart only beats for me and that I am his future wife so I have nothing to worry about." Kerry-Ann is the excited and fun one with a down-to-earth personality. She would stand by her friends no matter what the circumstances. Destiny is a rich, undercover, freak but quick to give a helping hand, and Careen is the humble undercover bed gal; everything she does surprises her friends. She is sometimes judge wrongfully by everyone but in the end they all need each other's personality to help each other get trough bad times. Because of this, they captured a lot of enemies in their age group, as the three of them have been friends forever. They all have something going on. They all are ambitious and successful at whatever they do and so were their parents.

Destiny's mother, Rose, is a psychologist and her father is a Homicide Detective who worked in Miami because the pay is better and their profession is better acknowledged. They needed the money so they could pay for Destiny's college tuition and to finish building their house. The decision was hard at first to leave their only daughter by herself but she was fifteen at the time and smart and had the whole community, her friends and Kerry-Ann's mother looking after her. So at the end of the day they both had to do what they had to do to get her through college.

"Kerry-Ann where is Destiny?" Before she could finish her question Destiny hit Careen on her ass.

"What's up ladies?"

"What's up with you, where have you been? We been waiting for you over on hour now."

"I had some things I have to take care of."

"I hope you didn't have a man in your parent's house."

She answered the question with an uncomfortable look

on her face and didn't make eye contact with Kerry-Ann, "So what if I had a man in my parents' house. I'm seventeen years old. I can and will do whatever the hell I want to do."

"Calm down. Careen was just joking I am sure she did not mean anything by it. You've been acting different ever since you came back from Miami and avoiding eye contact with me as well. What is wrong with you?"

"It's nothing, sis. I'm just stressed we just graduated high school and I have to start college in September. I was planning on taking a semester to decide what I really want to do but I cannot bring that to mummy. She is not even trying to hear that, she is working so hard for me and I don't want to make it seems as if I'm being ungrateful."

"I know how you feel but you know our parents have big dreams for us and we better bring those dreams to reality whether we like it or not." Kerry-Ann said trying her best to keep her in a good mood and take her mind off what Careen had said earlier.

"Back to you Careen," she kisses her teeth and turns around giving all her attention to the Heineken she is drinking, showing no interest in what she had to say. "You quick to tell me not to have any man in my parents' house."

"Hold on, Destiny. I never tell you not to have any man in their house. I said I *hope*."

"Whatever same thing, you need to start worrying about getting with the program; you need to give up that virgin pussy of yours. Kerry-Ann and I been fucking for about a year now and you still holding out."

"I need to find the right man; someone that I love and who will love me back for the rest of my life."

"Well, keep dreaming, there is no good man out there. I found that out on my last trip to Miami even if you find it there is always something or someone to fuck it up."

"Don't listen to her, Careen, she is just jealous because she was the first to give up hers to the handicap from next door," Kerry-Ann said as they all busted out laughing.

"For your information, Kerry-Ann, I did not have sex with him. I lost my virginity on my sixteen birthday."

"But you where visiting your parents at that time."

"Yes and your point is?"

"Your man is in Miami? no wonder why we never met him, so you lie to us you said it was the handicap who sample it first?"

"So what if I lie?" she asks timidly, I cannot tell you who I first had sex with so drop it."

"We all made a promise that we would tell each other who take our virginity." Kerry-Ann argued with her in an angry tone, "Take me to court then," she yells looking at the both of them with a frown.

"You are not right, Destiny."

"Shut the hell up Careen."

While they where their still arguing the selector announced, "All a the woman dem mek mi see yuh walk out now." Destiny and Kerry-Ann started grinning from ear to ear in excitement, they did not waste any time acting more like girls gone mad, than girls gone wild. They continued their madness for about half an hour until they come rushing back over to Careen who was in her own world and find the whole thing ridiculous and boring.

Destiny and Kerry-Ann were still trying to catch their breath when Careen signals them by rubbing her eyes and yawning to let them know that she was ready to go home. She whether to be wrap up in her sheet sipping on some mint tea and reading even though it was her celebration night she was already convinced that Destiny had already fuck that up so there is no point being there anymore.

"Careen stop the yawning, no man let me call Steve to come pick us up."

"Steve," Kerry-Ann signs as she listens to what he had to say.

"Can you come get us we still at the club. I will buy you gas Steve just come." she hung up and turned to face her friends, "Mi say him don't do nothing fi people fi free, him always want something in return."

"Mi a tell you sis everyone need money and will do anything now a days to get it they all want to look hot, too much MTV and BET."

"Shut up Destiny. Yuh so stupid."

"I'm telling you, Careen, everyone wants to be Americanize and the simple thing that use to mek dem happy and the things that they use to treasure they push it aside. When was the last time you saw someone catching some fish or planting some food? The gal dem don't even want to go down on dem knees to clean their own floor anymore. The bwoy dem, that we use to watch play football on Sundays, where dem at now? Some inna jail fi thief people things and some outta the plaza hanging out. When you ask dem wha gwan, their answer always the same " bwoy mi dah yah, a gaawn easy. Mi suppose, to get a visa next year" like dem fucking life should be on stand still until then."

"Mi see that you have some knowledge on life Destiny."

"Why you always try to disrespect me Careen?"

"You are one of my best friends and I would never do that, but what you are saying is true."

"Well, thank you."

"You're Welcome."

They finish up their last sip of Heineken and make their way outside of the club looking to see if Steve was there yet. They walked across the road finding the nearest car to lean up against, only to frighten them selves by the sound of the alarm that they set off.

# Chapter2
# My love has come!

"Hi sexy," was a deep voice coming from the side of the club. They all turn around ready to curse someone out. They knew that they could get any man that they choose, but they weren't the run around type of girls and didn't want to portray themselves as being desperate for any man. They pick and choose whom they want to talk to, at a time when they feel like it.

"There are three sexy women here. May I ask which one are you referring to?" "This one with the brown eyes."

Kerry-Ann catches herself from showing her expression while Destiny puts her hand over her mouth with the expression of "Oh my God!" Careen squeezes her legs together as she began to get moist in her underwear. She never had sex before, but all that reading, internet and movies can turn anyone into a pro - she was knowledgeable about reaching her climax and having multiple organisms and these were the things she wanted to experience with him. He walks over slowly towards them making himself more visible in the light. Apart from Careen thinking about fucking him right there she was blown away by his six feet two inch height. For a girl that never shows much interest in a man sure knows a lot about them. His dark chocolate complexion, his bow- legs and well-built body had her weak. The closer he got the more she melted by the discovered scent of his cologne and a smile that twinkled along with the light.

"Hi, I'm Troy Scott what is your name?" He asks in a soft and sexy tone.

"Ca" you fi get you name?"

"Shut up Kerry-Ann give me some privacy, you and Destiny," she said as she pushes them both away.

"We are not leaving you here by yourself," Destiny said.

"She is good, mi will take good care of her," he said gazing over at her. They hesitated at first but decided to grant Careen her wish and, for some reason, trust that he will do what he said and take care of her. They left but were close enough so they could still look out for her.

Careen continued to search for her name. "What is your name?" he asked again.

"I'm sorry, it's Careen." He extended out his hand to shake hers, and before he let it go, he slowly moved it up to his mouth and gave it the softest kiss his lips had ever given before.

"I like your name. Careen," he repeated it several times trying his best never to forget it. "You are the most beautiful woman I ever seen in my whole twenty one years of life."

"So you are twenty one," she said with a smile.

"Yes and let me guess how old you are without thinking," he said. "Seventeen, right?" She blushed without giving him the opportunity to notice.

"How did you knew that on the first guess?" You didn't happen to over hear my friends and I talking about celebrating my birthday today right?"

"Well you do look seventeen and I am also good at just knowing a person age maybe it is a gift and if it is I'm glad I was bless with it tonight." She smiled crossing her arms across her chest as she gazed down at her toes.

"So tonight is your birth night?" he asked.

"Yes it is," he took the time to glance at his watch; it was 11:55p.m.

"Well you have five more minutes before it is over so I would like to take this time to say happy birth night and to ask you to dance with me."

"I never dance before I have no idea how to."

"Can you put your arms around my neck?"

"Yes" then that is all you need to know. I will be your guide just follow my lead."

Careen couldn't help thinking to herself how amazing this man is and how could she possibly feel this way about someone she just met the question that scared her is it love? It was not possible she let her mind believe that all feelings would go away by morning. She was tired and had more than the usual to drink so her mind was just playing with her heart. They danced to Whitney Huston song "I *will always love you"* which was playing in the club. They danced for about ten minutes until she unwrapped her self from his arms and took two steps back staring deep into his eyes.

"The answer that you gave to me earlier, when I ask you about how did you knew my age by only guessing one time; I do believe that there is something more to it than that. I'm not convinced by what you said."

"Well have you ever heard what some people say about when you love someone you can tell and feel everything about that person without them saying anything?"

"Yes. So you are telling me that you love me and we just met couple minutes ago?" she asked, sounding curious as much as how she look.

"Actually for three hours and fifteen minutes that is how long I have my eyes on you."

"We didn't met," she said.

"I should say my eyes did." They both laugh even though Careen is feeling something for him she refused to tell him more than he needed to know. She needed to be sure before she decided to say anything to him.

"From the first time that you step out of the car, I been watching you. From that moment until the day that I die I will always want you where I can look at you. It is only up to you to change that. I will see you in my dreams when I am asleep, I will reminisce about you in my thoughts as I will see you in imagination when I'm awake and that is a promise."

"Nice lines, which love book or movie did you get that from?"

"Neither but from the vessels of my heart." She was dying with laughter only he that remain serious and feel ashamed as if he had just give her his heart but she purposely puncture it and handed it back to him. He was embarrassed and wasn't afraid to show it. She stopped laughing when she realized that she was being childish.

"Lighten-up, Troy. I was just joking," she said, but he still remains serious and for the first time since they had been talking, the ground is what that now captured his attention. With the most innocent look on her face she said, "I'm so sorry" and kissed his lips. As much as how pissed off he was, he didn't hold back to return the favor of kissing her back. She put her head on his chest and asked the question to make sure it was still the same, "you are saying that you believe in love Troy?"

"Yes I do and I wasn't sure that true love is out there anymore, I didn't knew that people still love like how my parents and grandparents did until I read about the couple that dies holding hands on their way from Kingston. I believe it was Mr. and Mrs. Shaw they both lived in the next community over from my grandfather." Tears immediately falls down her face Hitting the ground faster than she wanted it to.

# Chapter 3
# I last them!

Careen parents death was hard for her to get over; she had just turned fifteen when they died. She was Old enough to understood death but she couldn't understand why it had to be her parents at the time that she needed them the most. Her graduation will be in a couple of years and she needed them to be their watching and waving at her. She needed advice on who to date, career choices and someone to walk her down the aisle as well as helping her pick out her wedding dress. Careen reached the breaking point and stopped going to church and gave up on god; she hated herself and everyone that she knew. She spent months constantly asking the same question, "What have I done so terrible that I have to be punished like this? Why did you gave me my parents and then take them back from me not only one but both of them, in the most desperate time in my life?" Everyone was asking each other the question, why? But no one had the answer, which made it more frustrating and painful to handle. Camorra and Desmond were love and respected by everyone who knew him or her. Camorra was a gynecologist who worked at Kingston Hospital and Desmond drove a taxi in St. Elizabeth. They lived a simple life but, beautiful and filled with love and happiness. They were together before they knew what the word love meant.

They were born a couple days apart and spend their whole life together. They attended the same school, church and the Same activities and still couldn't got enough of each other. One Monday evening Camorra was working late, as usual, Desmond knew that and being the good husband that he is he decided to surprise her and went up to her work place. He dressed up looking as fine as he was for his age, the both of them was perfect together. Careen looked just like her mother they could pass for twins. Camorra did a good job keeping up with her shape by working out for an hour at the gym every day. While gathering her things to get out for the day she heard a knock at the door.

"Who is it?" Praying it is not one of her patients going into labor she was tired and wasn't in the mood to deliver any more baby for the day.

"It's your husband woman, open the door who else you think it is"? He said in a rough and sexy tone. "It could be anybody," she said with a smile as she opened the door and was blown away by the way he presented himself - so sexy.

"What are you doing here Desmond did you work today?"

"Yes I did" as he forced to pass her. "Mi come fi take my wife out fi dinner so mi hope sah you're not too tired and you are hungry." She wrapped her arms around his neck.

"Well I'm never too tired for you and I'm very hungry."

"Good let's get your things and let's go cause mi have a little toppings to go along with that dinner but that is fi lata."

He wrapped his hands around her waist pulling her closer to him so he could kiss her on her lips. "I love you girl ever since we use to share cheese chips from your lunch kit."

"She was laughing so hard she was unable to hold herself

up. Desmond caught her just before she makes connection with the floor.

"I love you too sweetie from the time I use to sit on my front step and watch your mother beating your ass, that use to make my day."

"I bet it did."

"Come on no man," he said sounding tired. "What am I going to do with my car?"

"Leave it here. I will take you to work tomorrow."

"Are you planning on driving such a long distance just to take me to work?"

She sounded concerned. "Sweetie cum inna the car, how you can murmur so man? Who tell yuh sah we going home tonight," he said with a smile she didn't bother to say anything else to him she knew that she would enjoy whatever it is that he had to give her that night. Her million-dollar Land Cruiser was parked in her private parking in the top garage where it should be safe until the next day.

"Which restaurant are we going to baby?" He asks looking over at her in the passenger seat fixing her hair.

"I have no idea"

"I thought you would have an idea since you work here every day."

"Sorry but I don't."

"You no go fi lunch a day time?"

"No the girls usually bring me back something to keep me alive until I get home."

"We will find somewhere," as he take her hand in his. They drove around for ten minutes and he still could not find anywhere romantic enough for his wife. She was getting sleepy and frustrated to her it felt as though they had been driving for hours; the traffic was getting heavier by the second with everyone trying to get home before dark. The last thing that she wanted was to sit for hours feeling hot, hungry and horny. Desmond finally pulled over and decided to ask someone, "boss man yuh know no weh nice round here weh mi can get some good food?"

As he yelled from his half-winded down window. "Yah man just keeps going up and turn pon the First Street up dah so." About three minutes up the street he see a sign attach to this beautiful small, place printed lovers choice, dem food good man" the man yell from down the street making his way towards them. "Alright thanks, man," Desmond yells back. He parked the car and went around opening up Camorra door. They walk inside wrapped up in each other's arms chatting and laughing at her husband's silly jokes. A waitress met them at the door, "Welcome to lover's choice," she said as she took the lead walking them over to the perfect table for two by the window. Two more minutes into their fun time and then there was silence as they captivated each other's eyes. He took her hand and place it on his heart she could felt every beat reminding her of the time when Careen was conceived, they made love for hours by the time they stopped they were both searching desperately trying to find their breath she put her ear on his heart and sing along with the sweet rhythm of his heart beat. He looked in her eyes as she looked into his for about three to four minutes letting each other eyes and hands speak the words for their lips. He finally released the air that he was holding in since he first made eye contact with his wife. He rested his elbows and the table leaning forward to Camorra pulling her closer to him, "Baby, I want to thank you for the most wonderful time of my life, God has created us and put us together for the reason to give love to people who needed it and to teach it to who is willing to learn. Because of you I don't know what it feels like to be sad, lonely, to need a friend a lover a teacher you have completed me and everything that I had ever desire and for that I wanted to say thank you."

"Darling you have done the same for me and more, because of you I never knew what it feels like to be cheated on, to be beaten or betrayed by a man and for giving us Careen for that thank you and I will love you in this life and the next," she said

Squeezing his fingers, "You're welcome my love." He sat up from off his chair, leaned over and kissed her tears away. "Come on baby hurry up so we can leave this place mi cannot keep that beautiful room empty and cold because tonight belong to you I'm going give you what you been longing for and nuff more" he said throughout his laughter.

"Maybe we can mek a Desmond Jr.," she said laughing back at him, " mi always up fi anything you done know that already."

"Well hurry up, you want mi fi help you eat?" He asks as he eases back in his chair.

"No" she said.

"But you a eat like seh you no have no teeth, gimmi dah piece a meat right dah so? He asks in a different manner,"

"No, why you so gravelicious? Just sit back and relax you self man," she said. Even thought he was rushing her to go she insisted on using that opportunity to talk to him about a decision she was planning on making soon. "Baby I know that you wanted to go, but I need to talk to you."

"Can we talk in the car?"

"No, right here Desmond."

"Mi tired man,"

"Pull yourself together and stop behaving as if you are two"

By him chewing on the straw did not make a good image of him at the time, in a sarcastically manner he answered, "yes madam Camorra Shaw I am hearing you." "I was thinking about moving to New York and open a private office I would make a lot more money so we would be able to put more into Careen's savings. You know that the Universities are much more expensive nowadays."

He pretended to agree With her while he searches for the

correct words so they wouldn't come out in the non- supportive way. The last thing that he wanted was to spoil a beautiful evening. He knew that he couldn't live one second without her and Jamaica was their home and he wanted it to be that way. At the age of thirty-eight the last thing he wanted was to move to America but he was willing and have to compromise and be supportive of whatever she chooses to do. Camorra knew that getting a visa would not be a problem and also for her husband because everyone already made him out to be just the husband of one of Jamaican finest doctor. He could care less of what anyone had to say are how they might have portray him. He was the one that worked and send his wife to school because she was the one that was smarter and would be able to finish school, that is what having a partner and building a life is all about. He was ready to give her his opinion before he opens his mouth, he made sure he chooses his words carefully. "Baby can I make a suggestion?"

"Sure sweetie."

"He take a sip of his ginger beer for the first time he wish it was coconut rum and coke. "I am just asking you to think twice about this we or thirty- eight years old mi nuh say we old, but we did made a promise to each other that the age of forty we are going to settle down, slow down pon the work and travel around the world just for vocations. Base on what mi see on CNN and hear on the radio the economy is all fuck up right now you might ended up paying more monthly payment for the office that what you mek and it might tek a while to start gaining your own patients baby."

"We are blessed with more than enough, darling. We should give thanks we have more than enough to put Careen through school and we have two more years to go so stop worry you self." "You have a point baby what you are saying is true I already have everything that I needed if I should die tomorrow I would be well rested because I had a wonderful life." He kiss her on her forehead and makes his move, "Come on, baby.

Let's go we have a mission to accomplish." By the time they get to the car it was raining, pouring down by the minutes he could hardly see where he was going Camorra was chatting up a storm telling him story and giggling as well as he was doing the same thing. She still gets butterflies in her stomach when he tells her that he love her they hold hands while camorra listen to the rain pitching against the windows, while he try to find where he was going. She uses her free hand to turn up the volume on the radio trying not to miss a word of one of their favorite wedding songs that was playing. They both were excited and couldn't help it but to sing along, "I *don't want to close my eyes, I don't want to fall asleep cause I'm missing you and I don't want to miss a thing.*"

He was yelling out the lyrics looking over at her she was trying her best to match up with his voice but was unsuccessful. Her smile caught his attention allowing him to lose control of the car, soon after it started spinning and he was unable to get it back into control he let go her hand to grab on to the steering wheel but quickly became nervous from Camorra's scream. He followed her eyes looking forward it was a truck heading towards them at a speed limit about sixty to seventy miles per hour. toward his car. The car was still spinning base and how the truck is coming either the driver was sleeping or he had no breaks because he wasn't slowing down. Desmond wasn't left with many choices, as there were houses on both side of the road at close range. He looked over at his wife as she did the same with tears falling down their faces. She braced herself back in her seat and reaches for her husband's hand and squeezed it as hard as she could.

"Camorra Shaw, I will always love you in this life and the next."

"I love you too. I will see you on the other side." The truck slammed into his car they both died instantly the news read that their hands were still tightly attached together. Two weeks after Careen was admitted at the hospital for severe depression and was on twenty-four hour suicide watch.

"Careen what is wrong with you?"

She was still hurt, and hated to be reminded about what had happened, especially by someone that she didn't know.

"Is it something that I said?"

She blinked a couple of times, trying to clear her eyes from the tears clouding her vision. She look into his eyes clearly when she whispered, "I am Careen Shaw."

He instantly felt weak and the most stupid in his life, "Careen mi so sorry I had no idea." He was so sad for her and couldn't do anything other than to cry with her. He tried to feel the pain and imagine what she is going through but was unable to capture that feeling. Careen walked up to him and fell in his arms, all she wanted at the time was to be held and he did just that. She wiped her face, and was fine again. Only this time she told herself that she would never cry over their death anymore as everything happens for a reason and whatever that reason is she will never know because she's done asking God why?

"Troy" " yes" he answer sadly, "listen I am sorry for crying like this it wasn't respectful for me to stress you out with my problems. It is not your burden to bear nor is it your pain to feel."

"Careen, I should be sorry. I was the one that bring it up."

"It is not your fault and you couldn't have known so there is no reason for you to feel bad.

"Yow! Careen sorry to break up your love conversation but Steve is here and him already acting like him no have no sense, so come on." Kerry-Ann said as she grab Careen by her elbow, pulling her away from him. She finally gave in and let him go while he refused to let go. "Please let me take you home." He begged

"No," she said without thinking about it. "Why not?"

"Because I don't know you. For all I know you could be a killer or a rapist," she said.

"A rapist, wow! Mi can't rape nobody you no see how mi lickle bit and mi nuh say mi wouldn't kill but right now mi no have no reason for that."

"So what would be the reason for you to take a next person life," she asked.

"If someone try to hurt you."

"Oh really," she smiled and walked away making her way over to Kerry-Ann. Without looking back; she waved and tell him good-bye. She was a distance away so he had to shout, "When can I see you again sexy?"

She turned around and shouted back, "Who said I want to see you again."

"Just pushing my luck," he shouted back putting his hand at the side of his mouth.

She was tired of yelling so she told him that he could come and look for her. "Which part you live?"

"If you were paying attention to our conversation you would know."

She hopped in the car in a hurry so she wouldn't have to respond to anything else that he intended on saying. While he watched the car pulling off he remembered that he mentioned his grandfather lived in the other community over from the Shaw resident. He was so happy he started running home so he could meet her at her gate before she went inside. He laughed at himself and surely believed that he was an idiot for running away without his car. He thinks about following them but acted against it, he didn't want her to thinks that he was crazy, he still needed to learn about her personality. Some female would properly blush at the situation while some would find it uncomfortable and sickening.

It was hard for him to do but he went home and prayed for the next day to come so he could see her again.

"Careen what was that long conversation about?"

"Why you love people business so much"?

"I just need to know, you was all wrapped up in his arms like him a you rass savior."

"Him seems nice" Kerry-Ann said nicely.

"Yes he is and no bother sweet up the conversation cause mi nuh tell you nothing,"

Kerry Ann knew better than to push it. Careen would tell her when she's ready and only if she felt like it.

"Careen did you see how Destiny was acting earlier?" Kerry-Ann ask

"Yes, her vibe is different seems unreal but mi believe say she just stress as what she said about school and all."

"Where Is Destiny?" Careen ask

"She left with the same person that drop her off earlier."

"Did you see who it was?"

" No, Careen how mi fi see a who inna the dark?"

"Maybe she has some secret."

"What kind of secret Careen?"

"Mi no know but people usually behave like that when they have something a hide."

" Mi no feels so because we tell each other everything."

" Grow up Kerry Ann this is not when we use to climb mango tree and play merry-go-around we are teenagers who are done with high school who have a life and something's that we are going to keep as secret."

"True that." Kerry-Ann nodded her head in agreement to what her friend had said.

As they pulled up at Careen gate she told Kerry-Ann that she would call her in the morning. She got out and ran inside to greet Mama Tee who was waiting for her on the veranda.

# Chapter 4
# How we met?

"So what's up with you? This is not like you to be so quiet,"

"Mi just want fi enjoy the ride Dwayne."

"Oh please! Just let it out," he said in a sweet tone.

She was nervously biting on the tip of her nails trying to avoid talking about what was on her mind but she knew he would just keep asking her. She took a breather and let him have it.

"I couldn't face Kerry Ann one of my best friend and I couldn't look her in the face and the other one that I should be there celebrating her birth night party with her and I couldn't do that either. The sight of Kerry Ann have me thinking more about you and I and how fucked up this whole thing is. I can't keep doing this to her Dwayne and to myself. The fucked up part about it is that I love you." "Destiny one of us will tell her when the time is right" he said trying to convince her that everything is going to ok. "Just, stop giving me false promises,

Dewayne you love Kerry Ann you never yet denied that so why you come at me in the beginning and mek mi fucking fall in love with you?"

"How mi must know say you was going to fall for me or knew then that I would care about you?"

"You can't even fine the strength in you to use the word love but care."

He released his breath and put both hand on the steering in frustration not knowing what to say so it wouldn't cause on argument. He is six feet tall, brown skin, medium firm body, long small dread and the most beautiful long fingers she had yet to see on a man. They met each other in Miami on her sixteenth birthday. The moment she saw him she was attracted to him, she was laying down on one of the chairs reading and drinking some wine cooler when his shadow stole her attention. She couldn't help it but to follow him over to the bar. Good thing the area was packed because she had no other choice than to stand behind him, which gave her the opportunity to check him out from the rear and fill her nostrils with a scent, that she would never wish to forget. She interrupted his order and yelled out to the bartender to sell her a bottle of water. He couldn't help it but to turn around to see who was blessed with such a sexy voice. She smiled at him grabbed her water and walked away pretending that his existence didn't matter to her at all. He forgot about his drink and ran after her.

"Hi beautiful wait up a minute." She decided to have him call after her again sure enough he did.

"Hi," he said as he tries to catch his breath. She stopped so he could catch up to her.

"The name is Destiny."

"Nice name but I rather call you beautiful" "why is that?" She ask in a lust-full tone "Because you are,"

"That is exactly why you don't need to be broadcasting it nor do I need to be reminded of it."

"I'm Dwayne." He reached out his hand for her to shake it but instead she rolled her eyes, bearing her weight on her left foot and put her hand on her hips. "I like you a lot," he said licking his lips "no you don't you just met me."

"Yes. But I know enough, your name is Destiny, you are smart obviously you are sexy and you are the type of woman who don't take shit from no one," as if he was looking for brownie points he asked, " Am I correct?"

She answered with a smile, " Yes, I guess you pass for now."

"So what are you doing over here in Miami, Destiny?"

" My parents worked over here so every chance I get I'm usually here with them; they beg me to come this time for my sixteen birthday I usually spend this time with my two best friends. What about you?"

"-My dad owns a tool warehouse so I spend most of my time out here helping him".

"Oh ok, so what about your mom?"

"She died during child birth." He held down his head as he always did when he told anyone about his mother. He had been living with the feeling of guilt; he blamed himself ever since he had learned about what had happen. His father had done his share of trying to help him understand that it wasn't his fault but no one had yet convinced him otherwise. Destiny felt sad she couldn't do anything else but to give him a hug along with a soft kiss on his cheek.

"I wish I have some sadder story to share with you so I would get some more hugs and kisses."

"Don't worry there will be plenty more where that come from if you play your cards right. I have to go my mom is probably looking for me," she said.

"Wait before you go, can I take you out tonight."

"Yah sure." He was surprised that she didn't give him a hard time but knew it is possible for her to think twice so he hurry her off and ended the conversation by telling her to meet him at Sunset Grill.

# Chapter 5
## Our first date

"Dwayne get up, get you shit them and cum outta mi rass house, whatever you and I have it's over right now." Tears rushes down her face; he turned his head away so she wouldn't see his build up tears.

"What the fuck you a chat bout it's over?"

He threw the sheet off him uncovering Destiny at the same time. She crawled up in a fetal position holding her knees as close as she could to her chest. Dwayne is standing at the side of the bed looking at her unbelievable of what she had just said to him.

"Destiny mi nuh left you how much time mi have to tell you that?" he began walking up and down in the house trying to figure his feelings toward her. He knew for a fact that he is madly in love with Kerry-Ann but he was obsessed with everything about Destiny; how she walk, talks, her touch was different, her smile, to him she was more beautiful than the sun set in the evening time, it was more confusing and frustrated to him how everything about Destiny amazes him but his feelings for her faded day by day and grew more for Kerry- Ann.

"Dwayne please don't go out there yet, wait 'til them gal dah go inside because the last thing I need is to hear my name all over the place and it would be fuck up for Kerry-Ann to find out like this."

"Mi look like mi care bout what people have to sah! He kisses his teeth and continued getting dress in a sports T-shirt, jeans and a Nike sneakers then pulls his dreads in a ponytail. He put some of his clothes in his polo backpack and gave Destiny a long sloppy kiss before he exit the door. Even though she was all mess up about the situation she couldn't help herself from reminiscing about the first time they made love in Miami the same evening after their first date. The evening at Sunset Grill was peace full the breeze was cool, soft and refreshing her all white, halter- top dress turned all heads as she enter the dining area to saw him patiently waiting for her while he watches the waves rushes up toward the sand. He was looking handsome on sexy in a white cargo pants with a casual Armani dress short. "Hi Dwayne" "oh hi, sorry I didn't see you came in."

"I know, you where too busy watching the waves right?" She asks with a smile. He almost tells her that he was fantasizing about turning her in all

Sorts of positions, massaging her naked body with his tongue and then make love to her until sunrise the next morning. "Dwayne, you cool"? "Yah man, mi good"

"You still didn't answer my question," she said.

"Oh yes, mi like to watch it vary much it give mi a feel of calmness ", he said out loud to her as he said to himself, "like I give a fuck about that mi wah catch you inna mi bed.

"What did you say Dwayne"?

"Oh nothing just talking to myself I'm not crazy I just do that sometimes", "Okay" she said, with every thoughts going on in his head still he tries to get up and help her get seated. She couldn't hide her gaze toward his chest and his shoulders. She began to day dream about him holding her, positioning her in all position with those arms, his hips looked amazingly strong and sexy she blocked out his words from messing up her mind she was trying to concentrate only on what was going on in her head watching his tongue moves around and wonder about the miracle it could created and how good it would made her feel, she was already heated and wasn't planning on leaving that restaurant before they went upstairs to one of those five stars room.

"Destiny,"

"Yes" she answers in a sexy voice.

"You okay"

"I'm good",

"You want something to drink", he asks gazing on the curves of her lips.

"Yes sex on the beach would be fine",

"And here I was thinking the same thing" he said lost in the thoughts of being intimate with her.

"Wait She yells "I mean the drink I was planning on getting one for me" she looked at him and smile.

"You know as well as I do that you don't want that drink?" She said, "and how did you guess that one?" he ask looking up at her in wonders of what she was going to say next. "Dwayne please you want to fuck me as badly as I want to fuck you." he almost choked on his drink,

"So you want to fuck me"? He ask looking surprise

"Yes I do", she cross her legs using her inner tights to rub against her clit trying to calm herself down, "how do you know that you want to fuck me", "Because I have never been so wet for anyone else in my life as much as how I'm right now", he was now heated as well as she was, he had never met anyone that was so out spoken it turned him on as well as watching her swallow every sip of her drink, he wanted to change the conversation it wouldn't look good if he cum on himself right there at the table. "You want to dance Destiny?" She couldn't believe her ears *"this fool a ask me if mi wah dance after mi done tell him what mi want"* She thought to her self, but he needed some time to think about it, her boldness was tempting but also had him concerned why did she want to fuck him so bad? Should he do it, and if he did what was it that he had to lose? He convinced himself that he will never see her again anyway, so might as well he go ahead and fulfill both of their desires, but he still insisted on dancing with her first. He took one last sip of his drink slid back his chair, reached over and help her up, "Come on, dance with me I love this song."

"Me too," she laughed out loud in excitement, it was one of Bares Hammond hits *"hey, little girl each time you pass my way I'm tempted to touch, your dress you wears perfume keeps me wanting you so much.* Her dancing surprised him but so for he realized that she was full of it, they danced for about twenty minutes until they went back to the table and decided to book a room. The romance began in the hall-way while people shouting at them to get a room, she could care less about their comments her intense focus was on one thing only and that was to get fucked in a way that would never faded in her memories. He manage to open the door so he could surrender to her, he loved the way she makes him feel and how she felt in his arms as if there were no rules and anything was allowed. He reached behind her and unzipped her dress, watch it fall to the floor seeing her naked chest was almost too much for him to handle, but it was no time to show that she was wild and he need to man up and give her what her body needs. His manhood immediately hardened as he felt her nipples pressed against his naked body. He was tempted to go down on her but remembered that they had just met, he didn't know what she likes and their conversation did not cover that information. Until she drop down on both knees spread her legs, unbutton his pants and pull out his ten-inch he wanted badly to ask what are you going to do, but the feeling was too strong for him to interrupt her, his knees was unstable so he had to make his way over to the wall and lean against it for stability. She slowly took in two inches in her mouth teasing him she could feel his body shake. She could tell he never had it done to him before she tries to deep throat it but was unable to succeed. She takes in enough to satisfy his need. For her first time she could pat herself on the back those movies that Kerry-Ann, Careen and her watched really turned her into a professional and even if she wasn't, Dwayne wouldn't knew the difference. He was tired of stopping his self from cumin' he holds her under her arms and helped her up, pushing her on the bed and took off the remainder of their clothes. With the feel of his breath against her private parts she was so turned on she begged him to stop he aggressively grabs on to her clit and smile after he had listen to her moans louder than she wants to, she couldn't help it but to squeeze his head with her legs when she felt his breath blowing on her. Momentarily he watched her body tremble followed by a sexy smile. She eased back down on the bed he position his self on top of her, with his hard dick directly over her palpating vagina waiting to welcome him. He kissed her lips softly and whispered in her ears " I love you so much" she open her eyes to look into his to make sure it was him and replay his words in her head to make sure she heard correctly. She didn't want to give him false hopes and she didn't know the difference between love and lust, but wanted now desperately to learn before he repeated it again and giving him a wrong answer was the last things she wanted to do for his sake and her. She sucked in a deep breath the moment she felt the tip of his hard dick presses against her private as much as it felt good she reminded him to put on a condom, she knew his intention was to protected himself as much as she needed to protected hers. Even though men were blessed with two heads in the time of sexual intimacy they often times thinks with only the one below their waist. He tried to push deeper into her she moans in pain when he tried to force in more than an inch it wasn't impossible, but takes patient and carefulness most men wouldn't even thinks about the question that he wanted ask her but he needed to know for his sake also because her walls hugged his man-hood so tight it felt as if the very skin was ripping off.

"Destiny I need to ask you a question, but please don't take it the wrong way."

"Sure baby",

"Why are you so tight?" She didn't bother to think about it.

"Because I'm a virgin Dwayne." Naturally he didn't care, but he wonders of the reason that could had prevented her from telling him before they got started, he tried to take his time but she didn't wanted to be treated as if she was breakable she remained in whatever position he put her into to prove to him that she needed him and everything that he had to give. As soon as his name leaves her lips and reaches his ears he began moving faster, she hugged him tight as her body tightens against his sending sexual feelings traveling through out their bodies fulfilling each other with incredible, unforgettable pleasure. It was her first sexual experience and the best so far. For him it was one of his best as well. She put her head on his chest running her fingers up and down his stomach. For a virgin she really gave good head she was wild and I love that she brought out a side of sex that I only fantasized about. Even the way she moans was exciting she full fill all of my fantasies and now I have to forget about what I said earlier about not seeing her again I will look high and low all over Jamaica because a sex like this is worth looking for even if my life depends on it, he said to his self.

"Dwayne why are you so quiet?"

"Just thinking baby where in Jamaica you live Destiny?" he asks as he rolled over on his sides staring in her eyes.

"Why, so you can be my stalker?" They both laugh.

"Girl please, I would just like to stop by and say hi sometimes that doesn't make me on starker" She knew exactly why he want to come to see her she, wasn't stupid, but she didn't care Dwayne wasn't using her and if he was planning on doing so, she was already one step ahead of him because she knew he was only after the sex. That was all she needed from him as well -nothing more nothing less. "Mi live a St. Elizabeth." He immediately felt sick and ran toward the bathroom. Curiosity allows her to run behind him. "You okay Dwayne"? He tried to answer but he wanted to finish washing his face, he hold his head up reach over for a towel and dry his face she followed him back into the room and sit beside him at the end of he bad.

"My girl friend live in St. Elizabeth" he said"

What! Your girlfriend why the fuck you never tell me this before!" she thinks about what she said earlier if he was in it for the sex it will be the same for her as well, but a person sometimes never knows what their heart feels until it is challenged. Now she knew that there is something there for him it might not be love yet but, something stronger than him being just a good fuck. "I forgot Destiny please don't be mad I'm really sorry", he said looking sad,

"You forgot that you have a girlfriend? Don't bother answering that because if you say yes I might have to choke you".

"Destiny I didn't totally forget that I have a woman but we are so far away I felt free and I didn't felt like I had to hide.

"So what are you saying every time we feel like fucking each other we should take a flight out here?" He didn't know what to say because that was exactly what he had in mind instead he changed the subject.

"I bought you something for your birthday."

"I'm not in the mood for any gifts right now."

"This is not just any gift I made it just for you." He pulled out a diamond bracelet with little piece of heart hanging from it. He was right- it was perfect for her and she gladly accepts it and tells him thanks. "Can I see your girlfriend picture?" she asks sounding calmer than before.

"Why?"

"I'm just curious."

'Sure in my wallet" " do you want me to go get it?" she ask making her way over to his pants that was laying on the floor.

"If you want to, no better if you go." He said she look at the picture and looked at him she felt ashamed, dirty, used, hurt, confused, frustrated, disappointed, angry, and most of all guilty the face that was staring back at her was her best friend. Closest thing to a sister that she will ever have. The girl that she cooks with on Saturdays, that she grew up with, who she shopped for on her trips to Miami, they cried and laugh together everything that two friends can and would do together it was already done by them, she was wrapped up in the arms of her love one the man that she hopes to get married to one day is the man that I just lost my virginity to.

"Dwayne get your shit on then get out!!" She started throwing his clothes and shoes in the hall way

" Wah mi do Destiny? He asks looking shocked at her reaction, she push him out and slams the door. She slides down on the door and cried. It was the first tears she cried over him, but it wouldn't be the last.

# Chapter 6
## I told him.

"Hello Careen wake up, how you can sleep so much?" " Mi a sleep with you, why you call me so early a disturbed mi fa?

Mi don't even seh mi prayer yet". Careen grumbled

"Whatever mi need fi talk to you, get Destiny on the other line", Kerry-Ann said. "She went to the market and left her phone, you can talk to me" Careen said. "I'm pregnant,"

"What! Are you sure?"

"Yes mi sure"

"How you mek that happen now when school a go start in the next couple weeks".

"I can go to school pregnant and take time off to have the baby".

"Well mi glad you have it all figured out, you tell Dwayne?"

"Not yet he should be here anytime soon mi have to tell him because him ass a be there side by side whether him like it or not".

"So what happen to you yesterday?" she asked Careen.

"Oh I had a date, I was planning on telling you and Destiny later on our girls day out, make sure you remind

Destiny because she has been so distance lately." Careen said "She been acting the same with me but mi nah really pay that no attention anyway Dwayne just pull up mi a go talk with him before mummy come cause mi no need her fi know wah a gwaan yet,"

"Okay sis see you later."

"Okay cool" Kerry-Ann said as she quickly jumped up from her bed and ran to the front door to open it purposely stealing his chance of ringing the door- bell. "Oh hi baby" with a huge smile on her face,

"Hi to you hotness, you look extra beautiful today you get dressed up for me" he pretend not to be surprise but couldn't hide his excitement. She was wearing a bleached mix color jean skirt just a little below her butt and a lady fitted wife-beater with a yellow push up bra. Her clothes matched perfectly with her skin tone, her outfit was simple so she went all out in accessories from necklace to earring to navel and toe ring to bracelet and anklet. "Dwayne I try calling you, where have you been since Friday?" She asks in on angry tone.

"I tried to call you yesterday," he said, she checked her phone and realized that he did about six times.

" I was sleeping all day yesterday" he remembered how much he loved her and couldn't tell her that the business that he had to take care of was him spending the last two nights in the arms of her best friends. "The last time I saw you was two weeks ago before you left to go on your trip, you return back on Wednesday and mi just a see you", he was the biggest fool when it came to lying he knew it and didn't want to give Kerry-Ann any ideas, so instead he held her around her waist and pulled her close to him. "Dance with me baby" she couldn't push him off or fight the feelings she missed him more than he will ever know, she latched her arms behind his back and they rocked in slow motion listening to one of their favorite songs *when a man loves a woman* he pulled her head back and gazed into her eyes "I love you baby, I love you so much", he said

"I love you too boo and I have something to tell you," he followed behind her as she held on to his hands leading him over to sit on the couch. He didn't know how he would have dwelt with it but a part of him hoped that she was going to tell him that she is cheating on him. Then he wouldn't felt so guilty about his nights of hot passion and love- making with her best friend. Instead the words that left her lips were the last thing on his mind "I'm pregnant baby, it happened before you left two weeks ago." He was even more excited than he thought he would be, but then he thought how would Destiny going to handle it? How could he possible stop loving Kerry-Ann? It has been a little over two years now and he still feels the need for Destiny? He needs to either open his own store in Jamaica where he can be close at all times to be there for doctors appointment or even to just to cook her a meal or go back to school and stop living off his father's income even though he works for him, it still didn't feel as if it was his. "Dwayne you okay?"

"Yah man",

"A minute ago you were jumping through the roof in excitement and then you just stop like you remember something important."

"Kerry- Ann come on stop worry you self, come sit down you had something to eat?"

"Yes I ate, I need you to take me to the doctor tomorrow I need to find out how far along I am."

"Sure baby" he said as he reaches for the television remote and started flipping through the channels to find a game of football to watch.

# Chapter 7
# Girls talk

"Wah gwaan mi big friend?"

"Wats up Careen I see you driving your mom land cruiser."

"Yes, me have to get use to it, I need it for school."

"Why you need it when you will be living on campus"?

"What about weekends I will be coming home and what if I need to go to the store or maybe I just need to go for a drive? What's with all the question anyway Destiny?" Careen asked as she sits in the middle of her two friends.

"I didn't see or hear from you since you left the club Friday and, this morning when you ask Kerry-Ann to follow you into town and she told you she was spending time with Dwayne you get mad and left your phone."

"Listen ladies" Kerry-Ann stood between the two of them, "today is the day that we talk about our problems share our sad and happy times, a time when we laugh and cry together if we have to. It is not the day for one of our little disagreement that always leads to a cat fight so let's just drop the argument and enjoy the cool air, sip our wine coolers and let all our problems out". Destiny crosses her arms and cross one leg over the other.

"You know why you so interested in this little Sundays girls outing Kerry-Ann?"

"Yes! But I'm sure you are going to enlighten me anyway. So go ahead blow me away" "because you love people business" Destiny said. Kerry-Ann kisses her teeth and turns her attention to Careen reminding her that she was going to tell them about her whereabouts on Saturday. Careen was day -dreaming so she gave her a love slap on her shoulder and asked her again,

"Ladies I had the best time of my life yesterday we should all sit down because this might take some time."

"We already sitting down Careen just get to the point"

"Destiny don't rush me!"

"Okay fine".

" I met him down at the river under the apple tree, by the time I got there he had made a bed and had some pineapple and mangoes all washed and cut up for me. I forget how peaceful and quiet that place is. A place where a one can always feel stress free. Anyway I have no idea how he knew those where my favorite fruits, but I didn't care too much to ask, I just enjoy the moment as he took his time to feed me every last piece including the juices from his fingers and his lips. After that we talked about my future and his. He wanted to be a lawyer but wasn't ready to go back to school yet; I was a little disappointed but refused to show it. It's his life and I don't want to scare him off with no suggestion or ideas of my own.

"So what happen next?" Kerry-Ann asks.

"What else do you think happened? She goes home to Mama Tee with her virgin ass."

"Actually I'm no longer a virgin Destiny, I fucked him and it was the best first sex anyone could ever have. After he share with me a poem that he wrote I just had to give it up!" They all were rolling all over each other with laugher.

"I enjoy watching his lips as the words make their way

to my ear" So how did you know it was the best sex and you never did it before?"

Well Destiny any man that can mek mi cum four times in fifteen minutes it will and forever be the best sex, until I can find someone who can break that record, then I might consider changing my mind, but I guarantee you that will not happen anytime soon. He was careful with me and took the time to pleasure and please every inch of my body including my little clit."

"So you fuck him right there under the apple tree?"

"No Kerry-Ann you know why you would think something like that? Is because that would be something you would had done," Careen said.

"Chile please just tell us what happen."

"We started kissing for a while until he asked if he could suck my nipples. When he get a good hold of it him deal with dem like him a professional, mi seh, mi wha run and can't move I was getting so close to an orgasm unlikely I had to invite him to my house not remembering say mi live with mi grandparents, every step mi take mi pray that mama gone over her friend I couldn't wait to feel his dick in my hands. Based on what I saw rise up inside his jeans I could tell that he was packing big time, girl when I open the door and find out that my grandparents wasn't home I take your advise Kerry-Ann and become the queen of the night and in my kingdom I rule!" They all laugh out loud holding on to each other.

"I push his ass down on the couch and begin sucking that bad boy as if it is the last thing I would ever suck until judgment day. There was no shame in my game thanks to the Internet - where I was schooled very well; he was pulling my hair so hard thanks to Auntie for sewing in my tracks because if it was glued in he would be paying for a new hair-do. I suck him until I tasted his sweet pre-cum he lifted mi up and kiss my lips softly. I wrapped my legs around his waist and pulled myself willingly into his arms, he put me down and in seconds he went down on his knees returning the favor when he grab a hold of my clit I literally cried out for Mummy. The neighbors probably said to themselves that mi really gone mad this time. He uses his index finger and inserted it inside me while sucking on my clit, I cum so hard my body was vibrating and I almost fell off the couch." They were laughing so hard Destiny fell to the ground. Kerry-Ann was trying hard not to join her. Careen for the first time enjoyed laughing at her memory of the evening. "He put my two feet on his shoulder and teases me slowly push it inside me. It was the best thing I ever felt and that is my story." Destiny was speechless she wanted the whole story not just the half she begged Careen to tell her everything but she refuses her grandmother always told her that when she is telling others about what happen in her life it is always best to tell half and keep half for herself. That way if they decided to use it against her it will not breaks her apart, because only she will ever know what comes next. "Destiny I have something to talk to you about so leave Careen alone" Kerry-Ann turned her full attention to her friends, as Destiny became nervous wondering what the hell is it that she have to say hoping that Dwayne didn't ask her to marry him. I thought the pussy was going to break up with her but he probably realizes how much he still loves her. Couple seconds later Kerry-Ann bused out yelling, "I'm pregnant!!" Jumping into Destiny arms she couldn't do anything else but be happy for her and to her surprise she didn't feel hurt, just angry and sick to the point she vomited on Kerry-Ann's bare feet that was half way covered with sand. She hold her up preventing her from falling on her face while Careen pull up her hair from out of her face so she wouldn't get anything on it. "Destiny what is wrong with you, why you a vomit like you have young belly?"

"Nothing Kerry-Ann maybe is just something that I drink."

"Don't tell me is something that you drink because all you had was some wine cooler which is like water to you because you always be the one to hold your liquor so come up with a better story."

"Kerry-Ann I have a doctor's appointment tomorrow okay until then leave mi alone please."

"We are coming to the doctor tomorrow, I will ask Dwayne to drop me off after I'm done with my appointment okay" "you don't have to come Kerry-Ann." "Wah you a talk bout we need to know what is going on with you, we are friends for life remember, she wiped Destiny's face and helped her up, come on you need to get some rest."

"What a gwan sexy"? Troy said as he pulled up and stopped at her gate and stepped out of his car, she run and jumped into his arms. "Wats up boo, wah you a do outta mi gate so early?" Careen said. He holds her tight as if he was her protector and takes pride in being it. "Mi didda look fi you yesterday mi cook and bring some food fi we fi eat but mama Tee tell me say you gone a beach".

"Oh Kerry-Ann, Destiny and I have girls day out every Sunday at the beach we choose to come together once a week and talk about the good, bad, fun and excited things in our lives."

"So what is it that is good, exciting and fun that happen in your life lately?" He asked as he gazed into her eyes. Before she got the chance to gather her words he steel her tongue into his mouth and begin caressing it with his. She returned the favor and become inpatient for her pussy to heal faster it is still sore from him taking her virginity two days ago. He slowly removed his mouth from hers and tightened his grip around her waist pulling her closer to him tilting her head back for a better gaze in to her face so that he could share his feelings through his eyes and word. "Careen Shaw my heart is yours, I cannot stop it from beating faster nor can I stop it from ache for you, I am in-love with your drams, your thoughts and your imagination. I am in-love with your knowledge, your ambitions, with your good times and bad times with your sorrow and your joy, but most of all I am in-love with you. She was dying with unnoticeable blushes all over her face. "Troy all my life I hear people said sometimes one bad thing have to happen for one good but in this situation I wonder if God has taken my parents so you could be with me, because with you and my parents maybe my life would be too happy it would be too fulfilled and that is not how life is suppose to be. All I know is that right now, in this moment, I'm happy and the feelings that have grown for you are feelings that I never want to lose. I will never feel this for anyone else, nor will I share it with another. I love you Troy Scott now and forever."

Dwayne:

"Destiny open the door," he yells through the pounding on her door. She was laying on her bed in her room reluctantly reading some information on pregnancy; She pushed the book under the bed making sure he wouldn't notice it when he come in. The last thing she needed was to give him a reason to stick around her. She swung the door open allowing the lock to hit against the wall. "What is it Dwayne?"

"Mi can come in?" He ask holding his head down while he shuts off his phone; without waiting for a yes or no answer he steps passed her and sits down on her bed.

"I need to talk to you Destiny come sit down beside me." She rolls her eyes and slowly walks over toward him and sits down.

"Dwayne please give me a reason why you come over here a bother me?"

"Mi no know how to tell you this but Kerry-Ann pregnant" he hold his breath waiting for a response instead she un- cross her legs and removes herself from the bed and sits on her chair in front of her dresser looking back at herself in the mirror still searching for her feelings about the situation. She is still puzzled by why she wasn't feeling hurt about yesterday when Kerry-Ann shouted out that she is pregnant. Today she is angry and confuse, she picked up the brush and start brushing her hair. She had a doctor's appointment that she had no intention of being late for. "Destiny you heard what I said earlier?"

"Yes Dwayne and so what!"

"What you mean so what, you no care?"

"Honestly I don't," she said sadly.

" So you a go leave me now right?" he asks sounding angry and frustrated, before waiting for what she had to say he decided to beat her to it and started off with reasons and apologies. "Destiny please baby I'm sorry I love you and Kerry-Ann I wish I knew which one of you my heart beats for faster so I could choose, but I don't, I'm confused and in-love with the both of you."

"Let me make this easier for you Dwayne stay with Kerry-Ann based on reality she is the one that is carrying your baby not me. I have money; I'm beautiful, sexy, smart and will be staring college soon so I will be fine,"

"It seems like you never rass love mi, you quick fi let me go already" his tone changes from sad to anger.

"Love have nothing to do with this Dwayne mi know say the only reason why you keep coming' around is because mi fuck you the way how you want to be fucked, this is my fault too because I should have cut off our little thing that we have going on when I find out that you're with my best friend."

"Destiny how you going to sit there and talk like what we did was just a thing that night we become one. I took something that was so precious to you I was the first to make love to you, we bonded, we connected sharing a night of passion with intense sexual feelings escalating throughout our bodies we." "Fucked each other senselessly creating sweet and lasting memories," as she cuts him off. "That was it Dwayne, not long before that you gave your heart to one of my best friend

"Mi can't understand this girl God believe mi, so mi love don't mean nothing to you right?"

"Look all you have for me is lust and I'm sure that is all I feel for you too."

"Call it what you want Destiny but mark my words that you will one day find the right word for what you feel for me soon".

"Ok Dwayne let mi take this time out to open your mind up to something and break it down so you can understand mi, do you ever take mi out for dinner?" He lift a brow and looked at her not sure what to say. She knew the answer is no as much as he did he decided to sit in silence and listened wondering how far she was planning on taking it.

"Yuh mute now? She asks, " Do you ever buy mi a gift? Except for the bracelet that you made for me when you first met mi only because you where trying to earn points to get inside mi panties. Do you ever take a walk with me or come over here just to watch a movie? Do you ever take a shower with me, cook with me sit down and even listen to my plans for the future? these are some of the things lovers do Dwayne and don't tell mi say you don't want people to see us together because dem two gal dah over dah so always dah pon dem verandah every time you come up here and you never think to hide from dem so you can take me out and go somewhere that no one knows us". He sat there trying to block her questions from his mind, he knew that she was right, but wasn't trying to let her know that.

"So wah you ago Destiny?"

"None of you business just gwaan home, did you bring Kerry-Ann to the doctor already?"

"How you know bout that?"

"Bwoy you fool, mi and her a friend right? Nothing that you and her had done that I don't know about."

"That with nuff a you woman everything oonuh chat with oonuh friend dem."

"Go home Dwayne," her body language was cold towards him

"Maybe you can come fi some later she teased because I must admit that I love having sex with you but I cannot see us beyond the bedroom" she smiled at him and tried to kiss him. Instead he pushed her away and walked out the door.

# Chapter 8
## Doctor visit:

"Good morning Tanya, I have on appointment with doctor Tyler."

"Oh yes Destiny good morning, just have a seat and I will let her know that you're here."

"Thanks" Destiny and her friends found a seat in the waiting area; a minute later her doctor reached over the desk and took her chart from the nurse. "Good morning girls."

"Good morning doctor." Destiny said.

"I'm seeing Destiny today why are you all here? Don't you know by now that the three of you shouldn't hang out together because when you do you sure act as if you're in primary school again?"

"Doctor you been giving us this lecture ever since we were in primary school only back then you use to say basic school now that we are heading off to college you should had said high school."

"I'm not talking to you Kerry-Ann."

"No, but you're talking down to us, good thing I'm smart enough to know the difference, because you are older and because Doctor might printed before your name don't give you the right to try and change us, not because we might laugh continuously that doesn't make us a joker," " all I'm saying is that people treat you accordantly to how you act as a young woman." "Doctor Tyler based on the words that might come out of my mouth, the clothes that I wear, the way I move my waist, the company that I might keep, apart from Careen and Destiny, the way how I might sit, the music that I might listen to, the movies that I watch and the way I wear my hair doesn't and will not diminish my ambition nor my knowledge nor does it hinder me from being a good person nor will it prevented me from being a great pediatrician". "Kerry-Ann sit down, all I'm saying is that take things a little more seriously" "Whatever doctor I just said what I had to, I have nothing else to say because it might lead to me being disrespectful to you and I don't want that"

"You just did, why stop now?"

"No I stood up to you, which is a big difference from being disrespectful." Doctor Tyler is a rich top physician who believes that she knows everything and wasn't afraid of sharing them with every individual that entered her door.

"Kerry- Ann you need to make your mother proud and that childish way of yours is not helping."

"Oh doctor Tyler, I have something to tell you, this might kill you which I hope it does", Kerry-Ann cross her legs with pride and sit up straight.

"I'm pregnant I'm not going to school September, the father of my baby is a Rasta all him do is smoke weed and sit down on the street corner all day where I join him every now and then I'm not sure yet if he is the father or not because I been with twenty five different men not to mention the ones that I been with when I'm drunk", Careen was dying with laugher doctor Tyler put her hand over her heart using her free hand to call Destiny to follow her.

"Kerry – Ann all mi can say is that God help you."

"Why you don't ask God fi help you daughter who suck

dicks for a living in America and been on drugs ever since she left the country, now you want to walk away doctor." She stood up and walked over to her, "your daughter graduated top of her class with all her subjects and got excepted to one of the top universities here in Jamaica, but because you think that you are better than your own kind, the school out here wasn't good enough for your precious daughter you decided to send her away with no friends and family to look after her now look what happened to her, a fucking crack- head and a cock- sucker great accomplishment doctor!" She was so angry that she was unable to find words to defend her self "Mi a go call you mother wait till mi done with Destiny."

"Great to see that you find your language doctor, you want the number?" "Get the fuck outta mi office!"

"No," kerry-Ann said as she move closer to her, "not until you are done with Destiny then I will leave, now get on with it," she walked back to her seat and sat back down and reached for a magazine and started flipping through it, the sight of doctor Tyler was no longer important to her anymore. "Kerry-Ann, why you did that to the woman?"

"Careen is a long time mi want to put her inna her place man, she always thinks the worst of every young girl that comes to this place.

"Destiny what brings you in today?" Doctor Tyler asks. "I was on my girls day out yesterday laughing and talking with my friends and had nothing but the usual to drink a wine cooler, shortly after that I begin to vomit more than I ever did before."

"Are you sexual active?"

"Yes" destiny answer. "Only one partner right?" Doctor Tyler asks as she removes the cover of her pen and position her hand to begin writing notes in my chart.

"I should switched over to Careen and Kerry-Ann doctor because I know what is going to come next after I tell her no, "No I been with two" She looked up at Destiny and stopped writing and removed her glasses from her face. Her reply was not at all surprising.

"I need you take a pregnancy test."

"No I don't want to."

"Destiny it's good that you know now in that way an abortion can be done as soon as possible."

"Wah make you think sah mi wah fi have an abortion?"

She smiled at her and said, "What can you possible become with a young belly at the University Destiny?"

"What I'll become is none of your fucking business. Go ahead and take the test because I pay you my money, so I might as well let you finish your job, but this will be my last visit here!"

"Destiny I'm just trying to be a mother to you and give you some good and solid advice."

"I have a mother and a damn good one, you need to go and find your daughter and waste all that energy on her, I'm pretty sure she can use it more than me".

"Okay fine - leave some urine in the bathroom and go wait with your friends in the waiting room. As soon as I'm finish I will call you with the results". Destiny gathered her things and made her way to the waiting room. After she was finish in the bathroom couldn't help notice the happy look on Kerry-Ann's face while Careen was jokingly rubbing her stomach. She thought of whom she would be pregnant for and if she really wanted to take away her friend happiness by telling her that she is not only sleeping with her man, but it is a possibility she might be pregnant for him. And if it is for Handy, what could he possible do for her? She was confused and overwhelmed with everything and needed only the arms of her mother.

Destiny:

"Destiny wake up baby, what did the doctor say?" He asks while handing her a cup of tea. She holds her head up and reaches for the sheet to cover her face. He pulled it away and asked her again "are you going to answer me or not?" "I'm pregnant but don't worry I made an appointment to have an abortion tomorrow. After I saw the look on Kerry-Ann's face there is no way I can go through with this." He sits at the end of the bed

"Wah you a talk bout? Abortion, call the doctor now and cancel that. You must be outta you mind."

"This is my life and I can do whatever it is that I please, leave mi fucking house and go home to Kerry-Ann, she is almost three weeks pregnant and I'm two. That mean say you fuck her before you came to Miami".

"She is my woman, what do you expect me to do?" He laid back on her bed uses both of his hands to cover his face let out a deep breath and looked over at her "Destiny just cancelled the appointment."

"So if she is your woman than who the hell am I Dwayne, your bitch?"

"I never once say that nor have I ever treated you like one," he sighed and got up from the bed.

"How are you planning on taking care of two young babies and go to school Dwayne?"

"Let me worry about that."

"I thought you used a condom that night."

"I did, but it broke."

"So why you didn't let me know?"

"Because I thought it wouldn't be a problem,

"Well I guess now you realize that it is a big one now." She reply,

"It is more like a blessing Destiny, just please don't kill mi baby I'm begging you!"

She tried her best to whisper her words it's not something that she want to say at this point but she felt the need to let it out

"It might be yours."

"wah you just say?" he was standing directly in front of her trying his best to calm down." "You know what mi a go left this place because mi nuh wah end up a jail dis morning, just do wah mi tell you fi do."

"Mi we think about it, she said and make this be the last time you a leave mi house in a daylight."

"How much time mi a go tell you say mi nuh give a shit about what people want fi say. Dem a feed me? Mi a leave but mi will come back when you cool down." He said, "Don't bother coming back!" He kisses his teeth, grab his bag and go through the door before he was all the way out side he looked back at her

"You want some ice cream when mi a come back later?"

"I just told you not to come back" as soon as he closes the front door Destiny throw her night lamp breaking it into pieces hoping that he was still standing there so it could knock him the fuck out, she run back to her room and throw herself on her bed screaming in frustration, everyone and everything was racing through her mind school, her parents, Kerry-Ann, the baby and most of all the baby might not be for Dwayne as much as how it would help her get over some of the guilt, she still hope it is for him. She wasn't intending on fucking up her career for anyone or anything and Dwayne would be the best candidate in this situation he could pay for a baby sitter and even take the baby sometimes. Even though he would have to take care of Kerry-Ann's baby at the same time, but that wasn't her problem. She turned over on her stomach and started to think about Handy he was cute and the question lingers in her head why Careen and Kerry-Ann always refer to him as handicap he had a fuck-up way of forming his words but nothing was wrong with him. Maybe because he looked white and acted shy, not like your typical Jamaican men, he was born in Spain as well as his father but his mother is Jamaican, he decided to move here to live with his mother when his parents divorced about two years ago. He said it was better in Jamaica, a beautiful place where he will always feel stress free and have a peace of mind. Depends on what you want and how you live. If you except living simple and appreciate life for just waking up in the morning you will be happy until the day you die. She reminisces on the time she proved to herself that there was nothing handicap about him. It was the Sunday night two days before leaving for her trip to Miami with Dwayne. She was home feeling lonely and guilty over the same shit she been feeling guilty about for the pass weeks, she decided against calling him because he already explain to her that he was spending the last two nights with Kerry-Ann. She tried to understand, but had no choice but to accepted it once again reality had knocked her in the face that when a man had a woman on the side, on the side is where she will always be. She was feeling in the mood for sex and the only man that she knew was wrapped up in the arms of his woman, which happened to be her best friend. She was wearing a matching thong with bra and red pumps; she sat in front of the mirror brushing her hair allowing it to fall onto her shoulder listening to the raindrops beating against the window. The feeling was too strong for her to hold back from running her fingers over her nipples, the dimness of the light in the room was not helping along with the soft romantic scent of her candle she bit her lips, spread her legs slowly apart pushing her hand in her underwear the feelings of her fingers rotating against her she was so into it that she purposely refused to hear the knock at her door, until she felt the breeze on her skin from the open door she hesitated from reacting innocent because it was no reason for her to be, her parents were out of the country so it had be handy she said to herself, who was fixing the pipes that her mother hired him to do or maybe Dwayne changed his mind and decided to come over. "I'm so sorry Destiny I just want to know where did your mother leave the pipes for me to put in?"

"I will give them to you, but for now maybe you can give

mi yours that is laying in front of you." He walked over to her while removing his gloves, his wife- beater was half wet with sweat, which helped it to stick to his body showing off his muscles. Destiny took the time to count not only six but an eight pack that started building up from below his waist. She never realized before that his eyes were sea blue the sight of him made her even wetter. "Destiny you sure about what you just ask me to do?" He now regretted the question, her mood wasn't asking for a gentle man she needed a ruff neck he knew he had it in him, and give her more than she was asking for. His heart beat faster as he watch her slowly rise up from her sitting position, he took a step back giving her space and him to view the unbelievable sight of her nakedness the touch of her hands make him feel light-headed and was unbearable for him to stand up as his man hood rose. She moved up closer to him removing his wife beater so she could run her tongue all over his body. He lifted her head up and began sucking on her tongue it was the best kiss the both of them had ever had! Before she was too surprised to concentrate the only thing her mind kept telling her is don't stop. He watched her take off her bra that was shielding the most beautiful and sexiest pair of breast he'd ever seen and then swinging her hips side to side as she slipped out of her panties. He quickly dropped his pants to the floor while she helped him out of his underpants. Handy couldn't believe what was going on, he'd always fantasized about fucking Destiny Woodbury but laughed at his thoughts, but now he knew that anything is possible. He moved closer to her and began kissing her again this time he moved his finger inside of her. She was wet enough for his satisfaction, but it only made him harder he thinks to himself that if it was the thought of someone else that was making her so wet or if it's the sight and the urge of needing him. All he knew was that she made him hard and wanted nothing more at that moment then to feel the inside of her. She opened her legs more so that he could go to work even better with his fingers he was more than good, he actually made her cum in couple minutes with his fingers.

"Take me over the bed" she whispered in a sexy tone. He scooped her up and put her down on her back using his two hands to pull her to the edge of the bed he dropped down on his knees and didn't think twice from licking away the sweetness of her cum from earlier. She moaned as he latched on to her clit now she knew what it feels like to stretch to the ceiling whatever control she had was no longer there to stop herself from screaming out, oral sex had never felt this good to her, nor did she knew it was a possibility it could feel this good. She tensed when she realizing he was getting up. The length and the size of his man wood captivated her. Dwayne was a baby size compared to this, he picked her up spreading her legs around his waist while slowly sliding every inch inside her. She wrapped her hands around his neck but shortly after she couldn't help from sinking her nails into his back and bite her teeth into his shoulder he could felt her walls tighten against his dick as he pushed further into her.

"Fuck me baby!!" she screamed. He brought her over to the wall leaning her back against it and gives her what she asked for. Every stroke send her to on early edge of a orgasm he sucked ruffle on her two breast in moments to bring her back over to the bed this time turn her back way as he pushed deeper inside. She fights desperately to keep the pending orgasm that was longing to be released, again he knew that she was satisfied and released his at the same time. After he had went to the bathroom he lay beside her

"Destiny, sorry I didn't pull out I shouldn't cum inside of you."

"It's both of us fault handy no need for apologies."

"I wasn't thinking about a condom at the time that is not like me" she said. "I only been with one person and I always use a condom and I always get tested just to be safe I did one couple days ago and I didn't had sex with anyone until now with you I can bring the paper work to you" he explained in a soft tone.

"Yes do that please in that way I don't have to worry."

"But it's possible you might get pregnant."

"Yes it is possible," she said.

"Destiny I'm a good person and I will take care of that child I wouldn't mind spending the rest of my life making you and that baby happy,"

"I know that Handy and for that I respect you, but I can't be nothing but real with you, I don't love you and I don't think I ever will. And I will not be with someone that I don't love. If I hurt your feelings or if I made you feel used I'm sorry." "No Destiny I'm happy you be honest with me, what we just share together I will cherish for the rest of my life and I care for you so much that I will never want you to be with me and don't love me, God will give me someone to love as much as I love you, but the difference is that they will love me back the same". She thinks to herself how humble he is, but is humbleness was just not her taste in men.

"Can you show me where the pipes dem at so mi can leave, mi mother want mi fi do something?" She smiled and took the lead into the kitchen her naked body has him thinking about round two but knew that he couldn't go down that path again with her.

# Chapter 9
## Our night out:

Today is Saturday it's been one week since Troy and I had sex. The memory of him on top of me makes me longing for his touch tonight, but more importantly having me thinking and studying the calendar because my menstrual cycle has never been late before. School is going to start soon and I need to catch up on some studying fulfilling my mom's dream of becoming an English teacher which comes with a lot of reading and writing the two things that I hate most, but I can do it, I have to do it for them I'm a woman that was made to over come the worst, with Troy in my life I now give thanks for the people that fight to save my life and do whatever it was that they had to prevent me from taking it myself. Careen is laying in her room thinking about her life and enjoying the cool summer breeze, hoping the day would move faster so she could go and enjoy Chantal concert with her man. As much as how I love Troy I need to call him and find out what the hell he is planning on doing with his life. He is crazy in love with me as I am with him, but I also need security. She takes the time out to glance at her watch it was 6:30 pm the feeling of excitement take over as she jump up to look for something to wear she knew she should takes a long time to get ready and to find something to wear, the last thing she needed was to keep him waiting, she looked through her closet contemplating on what to wear even though he likes to see her in a dress she decided to wear something a little different. She quickly reached for a jean skirt or maybe a tight fitted white jeans she said to herself with a pair of black pumps and a off the shoulder black blouse written sexy in the back, she looked classy and beautiful the look was perfect for the evening. She was all done with her make-up and was doing a last minute look at herself in the mirror to make sure everything was perfect, when she glanced at her watch it was 9:30 she worried that she wouldn't get there in time for 10:30 before she take a step to look out the window hoping Troy would be out there she heard his car horn beep twice, she ran out while she waved goodbye to her grandmother and jumped into his arms who was waiting for her at her gate. "Hi baby,"

"Hey sexy, you look hot tonight make sure sah you hold on pon mi all night cause mi nuh want dem bwoy feel like sah dem can cum touch you,"

"Troy please I'm all yours there is no other man out there for me." He started kissing her using his tongue to tell her a story of how much he loves her making sure that it was passionate and soft. " Baby stop before you make mi strip naked right here."

"Go ahead sexy mi sure won't stop you" mi know sah you wouldn't but I need to see my girl Chantal."

"Baby there will be many more Chantal concerts but this moment of fire between us may not come again."

"Troy stop it!" as she laughed out trying to take her mind off how hot he looked in a half-white jeans with a white long sleeved fitted short along a white blazer with a huge weed sign printed on the back and white gentlemen shoes and a white belt. He holds her hand while they drive in silence looking over and smiling at her every chance he gets. " Careen baby this is your night I want you to sit back and enjoy every moment of Chantal, oh fuck!" he shout as he pulled his car over searching in his pocket and looking on the back seat.

"What is it baby? Careen asked,

"Mi left the rass camera right there on the fucking dresser" Troy drive the dam car because mi can't believe a that you frighten mi fa"

"Careen you no understand mi want to get you face in a picture when you see Chantal because that will be a Kodak moment fa sure" she give him a love slap as he continued driving. Troy paid extra for them to get a front row seat she enjoyed herself and let loose into everything that Chantal had to say. "Baby you okay" "yes, but mi nuh leave until mi get her autograph." Troy couldn't help it from cracking up when Chantal stand in front of Careen and she was mute he was laughing so hard tears begin to fall down his face, she rolled her eyes at him and hit him in his head with her purse. She finally found it in her to tell Chantal that not only does she like her music but also respects her as a person. And how much she admired her gangster style and the strong woman that she is. They drive home laughing and talking about the concert. "How did you know that I like her? You have been spying on me?"

"Maybe" he said and then smiles, "because I always hear her music coming from your room at night when I'm outside playing dominos with your cousins." "That is so fucked up. That's a couple steps from my window while I'm there missing you like crazy holding my pillow when you could just give me on idea that you where outside, why you never come in?"

"No I didn't want to disrespect your grandparent's house."

"Troy I'm not a child."

"Yes baby I know, but it still don't feel right this is more exciting to mi, I like looking at you laying on your back crossing one leg over the next reading and humming to the words of her music."

"You are a stalker!"

"Well when it comes down to you I will accept the title with pride. He pulled up at her gate before she opened the door she once again decided to share with him what was on her mind. "Troy I have something I need to talk to you about."

"Sure baby."

"When are you planning on going back to school? The University has an excellent law course their why not come live on campus with me and we can see each other most of the time." She tried to convince him, but his mind was made up,

"Listen Careen baby I'm not ready to go back to school yet, I need some time to figure out what I want to do. Maybe becoming a lawyer is not the right choice of career for me right now. I never said I wasn't going back but I need time."

"Time for what Troy, you can dead tomorrow. Why not do what you can in this moment"

"But school nuh start 'til September you said mi can be dead by tomorrow so why sign up then?"

"You take everything fi joke." He laughed out loud throwing his face in his hand by the look on her face she refused to join him. Instead she open the door and was ready to step out when he held on to her hand pulling her back, "Careen hold on baby is not like I don't want to go to school is just that I don't want to go to the University of the West Indies. I don't have money for that yet Careen". She kisses her teeth and slams the door behind her. She couldn't help but to wonder why she is so upset. Is it because he wanted to do his own thing on his own time? The answer to her question even makes her more upset.

# Chapter 10
## First confrontation:

"Dwayne, where the fuck were you last night? The only time you spend the entire night with me is when you are leaving to go on your trip. I told you that when you left to go sleep with who you asleep with don't come back here."

"Kerry-Ann relax you self no baby girl and don't be accusing mi of something that is not true, just gwan go sit down man." He sighs and turned his back to her "mi did tell you sah mi want fi sit down mi look tired to you?" "No but you're pregnant". She puts her hands on her hip and stand in the doorway between the dining room and the kitchen while he leaned his back against the kitchen counter laughing and eating an orange.

"Mi have no time fi waste with you Dwayne" he scoops her up and headed towards bedroom.

"Put me down Dwayne me no inna the mood right now, anyway school soon start and I need some money to get some school supplies"

'Bout how much you need?"

"I just want some books," and in a sarcastic manner she said "and some personal items".

"So about ten to fifteen thousand will do" He said turning on the TV.

"About eight" She said. "Okay baby after this soccer game I will go to the ATM." "No rush."

"Hello come sit beside me" he said.

"You don't know mi name?"

"Why you have an comment for everything just come sit down man." She refused to argue with him so she walked over and sat beside him on the sofa. "Dwayne please remind me to call Destiny and Careen, today is our girl's day out and none of them had bother to call me yet. I know that Careen went to Chantal concert last night so she probably still sleeping, but Destiny had just simple drawn from us for several weeks now."

"Maybe she is just caught up in going back to school Kerry-Ann," he said trying to convince her that there was nothing more to it. "No man, she has some secret. It has to be something serious she was the one that never held back anything from us, but whatever it is, I'm willing and hoping to find out soon."

"Kerry-Ann mek mi watch the game no," he take her feet on put them on his lap and began to gently massage them hoping that she would just let it go, he couldn't stand to hear Destiny name comes out of the woman that he loves mouth. It give him the feeling that he despises more than anything else and the feeling of guilt he just couldn't stand it. "Dwayne you sign up for classes?"

*Thank you god* he said to him self while letting out the breath that he been holding in since the conversation about Destiny started. "No baby". "Why?" " I'm thinking about working full time to take care of the babies."

"Wah the fuck you just say to mi what babies?" She pulls her feet from his hands and stands up in front of him. "I said baby Kerry-Ann don't put words inna mi mouth." "Don't sit down in front of mi and lie Dwayne".

"I heard my self sah baby, if you heard other wise I'm sorry" He said gazing deeply in to her eyes.

"Yes mi know you would hear that but you gwan always keep in mind that the same way how mi pick you up mi can drop you."

"Wah all a this for now you love nag mi, no true?" he ask as he sat in silence

"I'm sorry, I promise I will never talk to you like that again," he said and kiss her on her lips. "I was planning on opening my own hardware store close by the university that way I can be close to you during your pregnancy." He carefully and calmly explained what he wanted to do for her. Everything sounded good and stable she put her head in his lap while she allowed what he was saying to replay in her mind and analyzing every aspect of it to make sure they would all benefit from it. "Fine Dwayne as long as you are doing something with your life I will support you and stand by your side."

"Thank you baby."

"Let me know if I can do anything to help," she said.

"Just stay beautiful, sexy and healthy for Dwayne Junior. She laughed "How you so sure that it's going to be a boy? " With all them seed I been throwing around here it better be."

"Okay baby whatever you say." Soon after she closes her eyes and fell a sleep he kiss her on her forehead and then turn his attention back to the game.

# Chapter 11
## Our new beginning:

The day was beautiful and filled with excitement as each of them received their blessings from their parents and grandparents and say good-bye to their relative. It reached the point in their lives for them to begin a new journey..

"Come on Kerry-Ann we are driving to Kingston today it would be like our girls day out only that it's going to be on the road, which should be fun." Kerry-Ann agreed with Careen as they packed their suitcases and bags into Careen's land cruiser along with their lunch that Mama Tee made for them. Fifteen minutes later they pulled up at Destiny's house beeping the horn and screaming in excitement "let's go Destiny we have to settle in our dorm by five p.m. and get our shit ready for class tomorrow."

"I'm coming why are you beeping the car horn and making so much noise for? You want everybody to know that I'm leaving" Kerry-Ann jumped out of the front seat running to her friend to help her with her bags "let mi help you Destiny."

"No I can manage."

"Well let me carry your hand bag because it's just as big as one of these Suitcase."

"Whatever! Hold this and come on before Careen start yelling again." "Wait! Destiny" Kerry-Ann said as she hold her hand preventing her from taking another step, Destiny was worried and was hoping Kerry-Ann and Careen would just talk about sex and old times and find someone to make fun of as they always do and don't bother asking her about who her baby father is, but unfortunately she was in a position that she had no idea how she was going to get out of it and Careen was too busy dancing to the music so it was not possible for her to tell Kerry-Ann to leave it alone. If I wasn't ready to talk about whatever it is that is bothering me.

"Destiny please tell me what is wrong with you, I know something is wrong I can feel it whatever it is sis we can fix it- I promise you." Kerry-Ann eyes looked sincere which made it hard for Destiny not to tell her what it is that is bothering her she convince her self that Kerry-Ann was too young and was not mature enough to handle it. But the real truth is she needed Kerry-Ann support through college losing her friendship now would be too hard for her to make it through school. "Kerry-Ann I cannot tell you, not right now this is harder than when we were in high school and we would sometimes break into the principal's office and white- out our complaints that teachers made or the time when you and Careen posed nude for the police to let me go when they caught me with the bag of weed this is more serious okay, so please lets just go". She tries to walk away but this time she holds both of her hands in hers. "What could you possibly have done that is so wrong? Kerry-Ann ask, in my eyes there is nothing that you could do that I won't forgive you for or understand your reason for doing so," She gave her a warm hug, "Kerry-Ann I promise you that I will tell you someday."

"Okay Destiny I will let it go for now." She pulled away her hands and walked over to the SUV.

"Are we going to leave today or what?" " Careen we are

in here can you just drive, shut up and please get us there in one piece."

"You been daydreaming for the last hour Destiny what's up" Careen said as she turned her attention to her, they been driving for the last hour listening to music and thinking about their personal lives. It was the first Sunday in two years that they spent away from their usual girls talk at the beach. Destiny wasn't in the mood for saying nothing anymore she just needed to tell them something so they would stop asking her what was wrong.

"Nothing is wrong I'm just pregnant." Kerry-Ann repeated "Pregnant fi who, handy?" Why the fuck she had to go there how can I tell her it's a possibility Destiny said in her mind "Yes for handy and I don't want to talk about it any more I told you that I'm pregnant and even told you who is the father so can you two leave mi alone now." She said while she adjusted the pillow under her head and sighed in frustration, her first serious lie to her friends she knew now that it would not be the last, but she was willing and determine to put a stop to it soon when she can.

"Mi sah Careen I had to confront the one Dwayne him the other morning and ask him if he's cheating on me because I have a idea that he is."

"Really!" careen said looking surprise, I bet the asshole denied it." Of course he did which man ever admitted truthfully to that question or less they are trying to break it off with their girlfriend are wife."

"True that still, but what give you that idea? He never spend the entire night with me only if he is leaving for Miami within the next two days and when he is not leaving he left about eight in the night and come back early in the morning his excuse is that he don't want to disrespect mummy and daddy by spending every night which is bull shit. They immediately accepted him the same night that I introduce him to them.

Talking 'bout that why Destiny and I haven't met him yet

and he seem to spend a lot of time with you?" Careen asked remembering that it had been couple weeks past since the last time that she had ask the same question, but now something is telling her that there is something more to it. What is his reason for not wanting to meet his woman two best friends?

" Because every time I bring it up he find some accused either him have something to do or somewhere to be his favorite thing to say is that we can do it another time" "okay he is hiding something for some reason" Careen said.

"I guess so but you'll meet him don't worry. You have any idea who he might be cheating with?" Careen asks. Kerry-Ann hesitates before answering. "None sis she said Anyway back to this, at first I wasn't really paying it any attention until the other morning when him come looking as if he just wake up, so I said to myself that it don't make no sense. Why would he go through the hassle of driving all the way back to may pen every night and come back inna the morning, at lease that was what he told me. But fi now mi left it alone whatever him a hide mi sure sah it will come out one day but mi nuh mak no man stress mi out right now if him a get something better out there I wish him all the best. Until him prove himself to be a good man and someone worth fighting for then I will fight for him but for now him can gwaan enjoy himself". Destiny never said a word during Kerry-Ann and Careen's conversation she pretended to be asleep thanks to her dark sun glasses it's hard to tell if she is awake or not but she listened as she tried to make sense of Kerry-Ann's speech. She now knew that she loved him, but herself and her education comes first at this point in her life, She wonder if she should tell her now before she falls deeper in love with him before they get married and decide to raise a family, but she realized that it wasn't that Kerry-Ann is too young and immature to handle the truth it was her that was too immature to talk about her problems. She was too weak and fragile to deal with the consequences that might come afterwards. "Mi have problem to mi gal!" Careen said with a huge smile on her face "What kind of problem Careen? "With Troy lazy rass." Really I thought you two were the perfect example of Romeo and Juliet the love that conquered all, the love that is understanding, sincere, patient warm and the perfect love of all," As she teases Careen laughs and softly hit her on her shoulder.

"Seriously Kerry-Ann mi can't bother with him anymore."

"Talk to me so that I can understand you." Kerry-Ann said with a disturbed expression on her face.

"Ok, all him do is get up, jump inna him car drove from May pen come look fi me when him no over him grandfather a help him, then him go to western union every weekend pick up money from his parents inna England, buy the hottest clothes and go hang out with him friends dem."

"So what is the problem? Kerry-Ann asks,

"What you mean, mi no just tell you?"

"Okay Careen you want him to work and go to school right?" She asked without waiting for an answer she continues, "maybe go to school with you, maybe become one of Jamaica finest lawyer or even a top doctor."

"Yes, that is what I want."

"You just listen to what you said right? That is what you want and I'm sure that you want the best for him as well, but sis he have to want it for himself too and is not what you want it is selfish fi you to say that, he have to do what makes him happy so him can make you happy, mi sure say him happy with you right now because him look happy. He is still young maybe him no figure out what him want to do in life yet all you can do right now, if you really love him and believe he is the right man fi you, is to support him. Every human being is different and men are totally different from women. Not because we got it together, know exactly what we want and work toward it. That doesn't mean they are going to be the same. Remember that your mother was a doctor and your father work as a taxi driver he never went to college, but that didn't prevented him from loving your mother, it didn't prevented him from being a good father and a good provider,"

"I hear you," Careen said as she eased back in her seat and took a deep breath "but are you listening to me?" Kerry-Ann asks "Yes" Careen answer in a soft and sad voice.

"Accept the man and love him for who he is not for what you want his occupation to be, you tell him you pregnant?" Kerry-Ann ask

"Why should I? Until him decided to go to school then me might consider telling him."

"So if he is not planning on going to school, then he will never know that he have a child?

"I didn't say that Kerry-Ann I just want him to become somebody, that's all" "You know what this not going anywhere right now because you are still mad at him for not listening to you and that is what you are making your decisions based on right now, but remember sah mi tell you this, true love never go away even when we want dem to, true love is very rare and only happens once in a life time. Some people are lucky enough to find their true love some is still searching while some will never find it. What our parents have is true love and what you and Troy have is definitely true love if you let it go Careen over this stupid problem that you made up you might lose out on the best thing that will ever happen to, you remember sah money and your big career is not going to bring you happiness years from now when you look at your baby all grown up and Troy is nowhere to be found or he is already married and has a family with some other female that filled the position that you should have been in. Then it is going to be too late." Kerry-Ann warned her.

"But they also say true love will come back if it is truly meant to be" Careen said sadly.

"True but not all the time why let it go now"?

"Well I did already I told him that it's over before I left, but he believe that I was joking" "Do what you want Careen but I can only be honest with you only because you are one of my best friend the truth is, you're being selfish"

"I don't care Kerry-Ann."

"Not now but you will years from now when you get older and need someone to settle down with, we can say all we want now because we are young and only give a fuck about ourselves but that will change soon". She looked over at Careen who could care less about what she had just said. "Stop over dah restaurant dah mi hungry."

"Maybe we should leave Destiny in here and mek she starve to death"

"Why you so wicked Kerry-Ann wake her and come on."

"Destiny!!" she screamed and beeps the horn of her SUV, "Weh the pussyclath you a call out mi name so fa"? Kerry-Ann laugh out loud as Careen join her. "The two a you is nothing but a waste of time you both don't have nothing better to do, I'm glad that I'm such on entertainment to the both of you, and I wasn't sleeping," she said as she step out and ran after both of them, "So you just did a listen to what we were talking about, what if we dida chat bout you?" Careen said as she opens the door to enter the restaurant "Who gives a fuck?" They all laugh out and talk as they make their way into the restaurant and find themselves a seat while they continued talk and enjoy their meal.

# Chapter 12
# Life on campus:

Careen:

It has been six months since I have been away from Troy and it's now killing me I miss him so much. I miss him waking me up in the morning, and coming over to my house every chance he gets. I miss our conversations and the way he say I love you, I miss even his very scent and he is nowhere to be found. I try calling him but his phone is turned off and no one has seen him. Everything that Kerry-Ann had once told me - I am living it I need to be held by him as much as how he needs to know that I'm carrying his baby. I never thought college life would be this boring and miserable. I need to be in his arms even just for one more time even If it is just for one night.

"Careen is that you? I'm sorry the door was open I couldn't help but see if you're okay. Why are you on your knees are you crying?"

"Yes, and its okay you can come in." He helped her up to sit on the end of the bed and then he sat beside her. "You're pregnant you shouldn't be kneeling down like that, you want me to take you to the hospital?"

"No it's nothing like that." She said with a smile

"Oh thank god I feel relief," he said as he exhales. "So why are you crying?"

"It's a long story I will talk to you about it some other time"

"Ok I can wait" he said. "So what are you doing in the ladies dorm at this time of the night Mr. Anderson?" she asks.

"Please call me Charles the sound of Mr. Anderson makes me feel older than my age"

*"You look good" fuck did that come out wrong she thought to her self.* She didn't want to give him the idea as if she was coming on to him it would be disrespectful not only to him but to herself as well knowing that he is one of her school counselors and a highly respected man not only with-in the school and the community.

He gave her a sweet smile two soft and gentle for a man she said to herself "Thank you Careen and to answer your question I was just coming from my office and I decided to walk through here to go outside for a walk before I head home the night looked too beautiful to stay inside. You can join me if you like." She nodded yes and he helped her put on her sweater and took the lead to outside.

"The grass looks beautiful but you shouldn't sit on it, it's a bit wet, let us sit on the bench over there." She didn't pull away when he held her hand. Why am I accepting this man kindness? She said to her self. "Careen you ok?" he ask as he sit beside her and for the first time he caught the true color of her eyes "You have the most beautiful eyes I had ever seen," She blushed and wonder why? Troy had told her the same thing a thousand time if not more.

"Thank you."

"You're welcome."

Charles Anderson is the sexiest most handsome man on campus he is about six three tall dark skin and the whitest teeth anyone had yet to see. He dressed unique his fashion left everyone with a puzzle mind including Careen, his hair always cut low and it seems as if he took all morning to shine his shoes because they were always clean and shining, even the way how he carried his briefcase was fill with style.

"You have a man Careen?" She was frightened by his question but she now knows how to act her age and handle his questions and conversation politely.

"Yes I have a boyfriend" she was unsure of her answer, but he wouldn't need to know that Troy was still my heartbeat and even though my lips tell him it was over my heart still aches for him.

"Can I take you away from your man?" She laughed more then she wanted to and decided to play along with him. "Well you could try Charles, anything is possible." "I like how you have an open mind to life careen." She felt uncomfortable by his gaze all over her from her head to her toe, as if he had never seen a woman before.

"You okay Charles?"

"Yes sorry to stare at you like this, but you are unique, even the structure of your face is different from what I ever seen before." She felt relief and understood his reason for his gaze. "My mother's, grandmother was Chinese and my father's great-grandfather was Asian. My mother told me that I was mixed with something from both side of the family."

"She is right," he said. "Do you want to have dinner with me tomorrow night? It's Saturday night, no school the next morning." he tries to sound convincing enough. "Sure I would love to," It was too late to say no after she thought about what she had said she had no idea why she said yes in the first place, but it was the answer that changed her life.


Kerry-Ann:


"Hello," Kerry-Ann answer the phone.
"Wah gwan baby girl?"
Kerry-Ann was laying in her dorm room on the floor with

both of her legs spread apart on the edge of the sofa accepting the cool sundown evening breeze to blow all over her body including her midsection.

"I'm here relaxing, school is kicking my ass but not as much as this little boy of yours."

"You find out what kind of baby is it a ready?"

"Yes, remember that you send me the money to get the ultrasound done last week?"

"Yes, I wasn't sure when you where planning on getting it done, mi tell you sah a bwoy" he said,

"Yes you did," She answers with a smile.

"Just make sure sah you take care of your self and cut back on some of your classes them." "I'm going to baby, you good otherwise "yah man, mi just pick up some shipment from airport and mi have some paper work to sign, it's a lot of running up and down but is my business so it feels good" He said.

"I hear you baby, let mi know when you can come pick mi up so we can start looking at apartments because mi soon have this baby." She said running her hand up and down her belly.

"Maybe next Saturday we'll have to start interviewing for a baby sitter at the same time."

"I know Dwayne" Kerry-Ann was not comfortable leaving her newborn baby with a stranger. She would feel much more comfortable bringing the baby to stay with her mother back in country, but she knew Dwayne wouldn't agree with it. He is excited about his first baby and needs to spend every moment he can with him. "Kerry-Ann we talk 'bout this before, but now you no seem happy is what happen?"

"Nothing Dwayne mi cool man" She said in a said tone.

"The only time you sah you cool is when you're not, mi can see you mouth long up now, talk to mi man."

"Well mi have this uncomfortable feeling about leaving

the baby with some body that we don't know it's not like they are a family member or a friend, but a total stranger."

"Mi did a think about it too," he said, "I was thinking that maybe the baby can stay at the store with mi during the day until you get home from class because your classes should over about 1:00 PM right."

"Yes, Dwayne you sure about that?" she ask sounding happy and relief knowing that once again her man had come through for her and done nothing but show her love and support more now than ever.

"Yes man I'm sure, mi just have to get somebody to work with mi they can open the store about nine and by ten mi can go in, that way mi no have to wake up the little one so early."

"Mi can live with that baby" She said through out her laughter.

"Just breast feed him before you go a to school in the morning."

"I wasn't planning on breast feeding him."

"So wah you did a plan fi do." He asked sounding confused of what she had just said. "Give him powder feeding all the time?" he asks.

"Yes, mi a young girl and mi still want mi breast dem fi stay stiff," she said jokingly. "Listen to mi Kerry-Ann cut out the fuckry and make sure you breast feed mi son at least twice a day, mi don't no why nuff a unuh woman now a day's concern about how unuh look so much."

"Okay Dwayne nuh bother with the lecture just pick mi up Saturday." "Kerry-Ann mi a get a next call hold on."

"No Dwayne do what you have to do and then call mi tonight."

"Okay sweetie."

Destiny:

"Hello"

"Hi Dwayne"

"Destiny is this you?"

"Yes."

"What happen to you, you know how long mi a try call you and a just voice mail mi a get."

"I know, I don't use that phone anymore mi have a new one now"

"Okay give me the number."

" No that is why I change it in the first place."

"Wah you mean?"

" I don't want you to call mi, don't try to come look fi mi, I don't want anything to do with you."

"So you find a man on campus? That is why you no want mi no more?"

He ask calmly,

"No Dwayne I found happiness. I'm content for the first time since I met you."

"Wow! So mi only brings sadness and misery inna your life?" He asks this time in on angry tone.

She hesitated before answering even though it is true she wasn't in the mood to make him feel bad. "No Dwayne but this game has to stop right now."

"Destiny what we had and still have is no game, I love you and you are pregnant with my baby how can you walk away from me and don't even think about keeping my son are daughter from me."

"It's a girl Dwayne you can see her," She said.

"A girl he repeated in excitement and couldn't help from laughing out loud.

"I know that you're happy as much as I am because you always want a girl." "Don't try to turn around what we are talking about I didn't call to share happy moments with you I call to tell you to leave me alone. I'm moving on and you are not a part of this journey and I almost forget to tell you that the baby might not be yours because mi fuck Handy a of couple days before our last trip to Miami."

"You fuck the handicap boy and have the nerve fi a tell mi Destiny."

"Well you don't own me, I fuck who I want when I want." Dwayne leaned back in the chair running his finger through his dreads trying to figure out what to say next all he knew is that he is hurting more than he thought he would.

"Okay Destiny mi will leave you alone but do mi one favor."

"What is that?"

"When the baby born I want a DNA test and if the child is mine don't keep her away from me, I want to be there for her mi want her fi know sah mi a her father and fi now mi will still pay fi your doctor's appointment and mi we buy ever thing she want just give mi the list when you ready."

"Mi can do that but if she know who her father is Dwayne Kerry-Ann will find out about you and I." He hadn't thought about that, he was just following the rules that his father had told him that he should always be there for his children even if he wasn't sure if he is the father are not, that is something he will never forget.

"We will work on that when it comes but fi right now mi will take care of you and her"

"Okay Dwayne and thank you."

"You don't have to thank mi Destiny just doing a mans work." *click* "hello Dwayne." First time hanging up without saying good-bye and he accepted my wishes for the first time. Destiny was sad a part of her love him more than before because he had prove to her not only once but on several occasion of how responsible and mature he can be and how much he has changed. She now opened a place in her heart to love and respect him more than before, but she knew he was meant for Kerry–Ann. They were one of the perfect couple and the love that they share is not easily broken by anyone.

Once again she felt lonely and needed a man to call her own, even though she had a strong feeling that love is near a part of her still believe that a good man is hard to find it's not every day someone find a good man nor fell in love with their true soul mate, she started to cry this time harder than she had ever cried.

# Chapter 13
## We are all grown up:

Destiny:

"Good morning Dr. D's office how may I help you?"

"Hi, good morning may I speak with Destiny?"

"Who?" The receptionist shouted from the other end of the phone line.

"I'm sorry Dr. D's" " just one moment please" the receptionist said.

"This is Dr. D's how may I help you?"

"You rass you a so when unuh turn big shot unuh change unuh name to." Destiny and Careen started screaming in excitement they haven't spent any time together since their graduation, they all been busy searching for work in their new careers and opening their own offices.

"How are you Destiny and that baby girl?"

"I have to say I'm blessed with no complaints. I reached where I was fighting to get to, even though the journey was long and hard now I can put my feet up and say I did it, so how is your husband?" Destiny asks.

"Charles is doing fine, I wish I could say that 'bout our

sex life. I been missing Troy like crazy even more these last couple months I can still feel his dick rubbing against my walls. I still love him so much I haven't spoken to him since I told him it was over, he haven't met lacy yet, I try connecting his grandfather and some other family member of his to see if they know where he is. They said he left about a year after I did. He calls and visits sometimes, but would never say where he was staying."

"You remember that little lesson that Kerry-Ann taught you when you wanted to break up with him because he wasn't ready for school?" She wiped her tears then answer yes.

"Stop crying Careen he will come back if it's meant to be I know that he miss you too sis as much as you do, you hear from Kerry-Ann?" Destiny asks quickly trying to change the subject to something less pain full for her friend to talk about.

"Yes she is getting married in couple months and wants us to be brides maids. She said she's been trying to call you but no answer" Careen said.

Destiny is still living with the guilt of sleeping with Dwayne now more than ever because not only had he been her secret lover but also the father of her first born. "You ok Destiny?"

" Yes, I was just thinking about something" Destiny now knew that she was right Dwayne really does love Kerry-Ann and happy that she decided to let him go nine years ago or else she would still be the woman on the side. She had relationships off and on but none of them lasted for more than a month, She needs a man who wants a serious relationship. Most of whom she has been with are, either married and lied about it, or just looking for a good time. She decided to post her profile on the Internet that one of her co-workers introduced to her. From the minute she posted it men have been blowing up her page with messages, but none have yet caught her attention. She needs someone that is successful and has the same ambitions and intelligence as her. Most of the men on the date line are half naked just showing off muscle and when she reads their profile it's always been the same, just a bunch of nonsense.

Careen:

"Good evening mummy."

"Hi baby how was your day, was the driver careful driving you this morning?" "Yes mummy, can I go lay down before dinner mi tired?" lacy ask as she rub her eyes and remove her shoes and socks.

"Yes darling but shower first you hear me!" She shouted making sure that she heard what she had said.

"Yes ma'am!" Lacy shouted back.

While lacy run off to take a shower Careen was dishing out some food to eat not even bother to wait for Charles because for the last eight years every evening he find some reason not to made it home on time for dinner. While she was doing so the tears started to roll down her face again the loneliness sank in. The memories of her parents started flashing in front of her eyes, how happy they were together and how strong and sweet their love was, and the memories of Troy only made it worst? She lost her appetite and covered up her plate and went to see if lacy was okay. Lacy was fast asleep on her back. Careen leaned over and give her a kiss, The remaining tears makes it way down her cheeks and fell on Lucy's forehead as she remember Troy's face. Lacy resemblance of him is far too much for her to keep his handsome face from running through her mind even if she wanted to. She misses everything about him, especially their communication and the way he use to take time out just to make her laugh. She couldn't help but wonder what if he is married and has a family of his own. What if he doesn't love her anymore and is not willing to complicate his life for her? What if he believes that what they had was just childish and immature? Those questions linger in her head until she takes a shower and fell into a deep sleep beside her daughter.

Kerry-Ann:

"Hi sunshine."

"Mornin' Dwayne."

"Why you say it like mi a the last person you want to wake up beside of?" "Bwoy please even though you have the worst morning breath and you always have you hand inna you ass there is still no one out there that I would rather wake up beside of but you ".

"Ya but you love me though" he said with a smile.

"Yes I do that is why mi can't wait to say I do and proudly change my name to Mrs. Clark" "in my eyes you were and always will be Miss Clarke darling. She smiles and kisses his lips, unsure whether to ask the question that she wanted to ask for weeks.

"Baby I have one question and all I want is the truth," she said.

"Sure baby wats up?" he asks as always worried of what her question might be.

"I notice that you left every evening for about three hours or more and every weekend for at lease half a day. Are you cheating on me? And please think about that question before you answer me" she said.

"You check how long mi gone to?" he ask sounding sarcastic Kerry-Ann was looking sexier than before in a black lace thong and matching bra complements of Victoria's Secret. Her pair of sliver stead that Dwayne brought for her last birthday go perfectly with her hair style a long wrap that was laying down her back, she leaned her back against the head board, half way covered with the sheet looking at Dwayne whose back was turned to her positioning himself on his right side.

"Dwayne look pon mi when mi a chat to you." He turned around." No mi nuh cheat pon you, please leave me alone so mi can get some more sleep." "Okay so where did you go?"

She asks with no intention on giving up until he tells her the truth.

*How can I tell the woman that I'm going to marry to in a couple of months that I went to visit my daughter and that her mother is Destiny I could but only if mi ready fi dead, god please help mi, the only way to get out of this is for me to turn it around on her I hope it work this time and sorry god to ask you to help me with a lie but I love this woman and I don't want to lose her so please help me out on this one"* He said to himself.

"Kerry-Ann why you always a stress me out with stupid shit that you have no proof of, you a cheat pon mi?" he asks, even though he know that's a stupid question it's the only way she would leave it alone at lease for now.

"No"

"So why you always a worry 'bout me, why you just can't believe sah mi love you and leave it at that mi a man that mean sah a no every move mi mek mi a go tell you weh mi a go sometimes when you hang with your friends dem mi no pressure you man so stop acting so insecure Kerry-Ann, now leave me alone." He pulled the sheet over his head in frustration and pretend to be a sleep while she sat there looking surprised as he whispered low enough so she wouldn't hear, "Thank you god."

"Dwayne I'm sorry okay, do you mind taking Dwayne Jr to his soccer practice I have to stop by the office to pick up some paperwork so I can get it done tomorrow after church. And it has to be now because I'm meeting with the girls to go over some wedding details so I don't want to wait until last minute."

"Ok Kerry-Ann. Is he ready?"

"I'm not sure, I didn't hear him from morning' him probably still sleeping."

"I'll get him ready and mek him something fi eat and stay with him until practice over." "Okay hon" She said with a smile, before she could finish thanking him Dwayne yelled out in surprise "oh shit!"

"Baby what is the matter with you?"

"Oh sorry to frighten you I remember something. I have to meet mi friends dem fi a drink and talk 'bout some wedding staff."

"Oh really?"

"Yes dear." Kerry –Ann was laughing to herself wishing that they would open a school to teach men how to lie. She knew better than anyone that Dwayne of all people is not going to sit around with his friends and discuss wedding ideas. And the yes-dear part just messed up the whole lying process. The only time he said yes dear is when I'm putting on some good wine pon him and I could ask the fool anything and him would sah yes dear maybe I should wait until I was fucking him and ask if he is cheating on mi. I'm sure the idiot would shout out yes dear! Dwayne followed her eyes for any kind of reaction because he knew that he really had to take Dasrine to her dance class Destiny is working overtime and is really depending on him to do it for her. The only option was to pick her up on his way to D.J practice and drop her off first and then pick her up before his son is done- his plan was perfect.

"D.J get ready and come eat something mi a bring you a practice today."

"Okay daddy." Dwayne JR that every one decided to call D.J is a wonderful and humble nine year old he got everything from his father from his bow legs to the color of his eyes. His dread is small and long just like his dad's. Kerry-Ann started to grow his hair since he was a baby now it's in his back he is very polite and respectful, not only to his parents, but to everyone around him even in his age group and younger he is a blessing to the both of them. Dasrine, however looked just like her mother. Destiny knew that is the reason why others in the community doesn't know for sure that Dwayne is Dasrine father but she know that they question it among themselves why he spend so much time with her?

# Chapter 14
## Girl's day out:

"Hi Kerry-Ann."

"What's going on Careen, Destiny how you look so hot today?" Careen ask jokingly,

"Mi always looks hot," She replies as she takes her seat at the table. Thanks for meeting me here ladies" Kerry-Ann said taking a sip of her lemon and water.

"No problem what are friends for?" Careen said.

"This place is beautiful from the high ceilings to the tall windows Careen notice as she looked around in amazement. She always wanted to open a restaurant. That was one of Troy and her plans but all of that was on hold because she thought it wouldn't be the same without him around.

"So how are you Mrs. Anderson long time no see, a little skinnier, but you still look good."

"Thanks Kerry-Ann, I have to keep myself at a certain weight for my husband."

Kerry-Ann put her hands on the table and leaned forward looking concern

"I wonder why? You have a child and a woman with a lot of responsibility who might gain a few pounds and you shouldn't have to look like you a weed head to suit his ass. Mi gain weight and if Dwayne don't like it him can gwan go find himself a Miss. Bones because as what my girl Lady Saw say *I'm not the world most prettiest, I wasn't born with a super model shape but I'm beautiful so walk with grace and so with that grace I will walk,"* they all laughed out loud and gave each other high fives.

"With all those rules that he is laying down I hope he is a king in the bed room," Kerry-Ann said as she take another sip of her lemon and water. Careen rolled eyes "Girl please! Most people pray to be rich, to have big houses and cars; all I pray for is one night of some good fucking. Not even one night but couple hours lord knows it would do me well for all the years I been missing" Kerry-Ann relaxed and let out a deep breath, "So you are saying that your sex life with Charles is not good?"

"Yes that is what I'm saying not that it's not even good but we don't have a sex life." Kerry-Ann was confused "What do you mean?"

"Mi means sah the man don't want to fuck me Kerry-Ann."

"So why you no tek man pon him you idiot a beautiful girl like you can sit down a stress out you self over sex the way how dem a Jamaican man yah so horny."

"It's not that simple I love him, and I'm his wife that means something to me." "No you don't you love Troy. You love the idea of loving Charles so don't give me that bull shit."

"Maybe you're right, I even ask him for oral sex and his response was that he don't believed in it, as if it was a culture or something of that sort for him to believe in. Anyway I finally convinced him one evening after he come home from work I spend the whole evening pampering myself from massaging my skin with bath oil to soaking in bubble bath to relax my muscles and slip into one of my sexy lingerie and a high heel pumps, put on some love music, turn it down low as well as some scented candle to set the mood in the bed room. He walk in the room and I went to help him loosen his tie help him undress and give him a bath after I was done with him in the bathroom and walk him over to the bed I didn't restraint my self from giving him oral sex, his little 6 inch reluctantly hardens but I was willing to work with it at that point I would work with anything all I needed was some fuck enough to make me cum. My body becomes hot and my pussy reacts to the sound of his moaning I watch his toes curled up so I knew I was doing a job well done I was down and dirty ready to get some he rolled me over on my back and my heart begin pounding he started licking my nipples I wanted to screamed out and tell him to suck it harder. I have no idea what he was doing I wanted so badly to push him off and tell him forget it but I stayed calm he started kissing me down to my stomach I rise my hips letting him know that I need his tongue to connect with my clit, he makes his way down there and I wish he never did instead of laying there upset about the situation I tell him what I want, and how I want it with no sign of caring what I suggested to him he went back down there then a moment later I didn't feel his mouth any where on my body. I thought maybe he was trying to figure out what to do next until I heard him snoring I push the pussy-hole off me so hard him fell to the floor not only was he incapable of fucking me with his dick but with his tongue as well."

Destiny looked sad as well as Kerry-Ann for their friend.

"I feel it for you sis." said Destiny in a pitiful voice "I feel it for myself that night I was so wet you could catch my juice with a cup I was so lonely and frustrated I started to cry, I know the problem isn't me, I try every possible thing if this is the only sin that will close heaven's gates on me for cheating on my husband and breaking our vows then so be it because I just change my mind of respecting my vows." Careen shakes her head as she wonders what could be wrong with her husband.

"Don't worry my dear you just need to find a good worker

man that can tear down your walls so that you are unable to walk for days," Kerry-Ann jokes.

"So how are things with you and Dwayne?" Asked Careen.

"Okay, so far there is no major issues to complain about yet", she put on a big smile as she gets ready to share what happen between she and Dwayne the night before with her friends. Only that this morning he tried to play that flip shit game on mi" out of curiosity Destiny asked "What are you talking about?"

"I ask the idiot if him a cheat pon mi right ask me why him get all mad and ask mi if mi a cheat pon him, him should have known that mi too smart fi that stupid play out game, but mi make him believe sah him little game work."

"I not even going to bother ask you anything Destiny cause mi never see you with a man you a lesbian are something?"

"Shut up Kerry-Ann no I'm not a lesbian and who I fuck is my business!"

"So why you always come to our get together since you never have anything to talk about you been doing this for years."

"Kerry-Ann listen I don't talk about anything because I don't have a man, at one point in my life I would call a friend that I met during college, when I wasn't with you two I was with him but I cut that off about a year ago. Now I'm looking for someone that I can settle down with because I'm not getting any younger." "Since you two use to hang out so much how come you never spoke of him are bring him around?" Careen asks. "As I said he was just a friend that happens to give me more than just a ear when I'm having a bad day" Destiny said sounding angry. "If he was good enough for you to had sex with him how come he wasn't good enough to be your personal man" "he's married" Destiny said as she take a sip of her wine cooler and take in a deep breath "you're such a bitch Destiny" Careen said. "Please tell me something that I don't know"

Destiny reply. Destiny nervously answers her phone. "Where are you?" Dwayne asks. "Mi out with Kerry-Ann and Destiny what is it?" "Mi pick up Dasrine from her dance class should I keep her 'till you get home?" "Yes" Destiny answer as she look over at Kerry-Ann to see her expression. But she was busy searching through her packet-book for something that seems to be very important. " Thought you were working over time today" "yes, but mi fi get sah mi have to meet with my friends". "You want to hang out with mi later?" "No! Mi stop fucking you fi years now and I have no interest in going back there with you". "Okay, you gwan play hard fi get" Dwayne said. " Mi soon come home just keep her 'till mi get there. Okay." Destiny quickly presses the end button before Kerry- Ann leaned over and sees Dwayne's name appear on the screen. Destiny wanted to ask Kerry-Ann a question every time they met for their girls day out, she knew that it's a question that she would have to ask eventually and this seems like a perfect time for it she take in some air and go for it.

"Kerry-Ann would you break up with Dewayne if you find out that he's cheating on you?"

"It depends on how severe the situation is, like if he cheats with one of you guys or if he's having a long term relationship with another woman, then mi would have no choice but to let him lose but if it's only a one night stand then no, as long as him don't have no one a call mi house and try to disrespected mi outta street then mi good." "Why is a one night stand okay?" Destiny asks as she drew herself closer to the table to get the full details. "Okay listen and take notes if you want, Dwayne and I have a son, we build a beautiful house together and share a loving past and present that is filled with love and happiness and to how things look we might even have a better future. Why should I leave him and walk away from all that we earn during our years together he had proven himself to be a good man and a good provider and he love and cherishes me. Men are going to be men not all of them but you have some that will continued to cheat even if they get sick from the thought of it, a lot of women think that their man will change because they said I love you or I do on their wedding day while some say if a man love you they will never cheat that is a lie. A man can love you unconditionally and still feel the need to fuck another pussy from time to time. Now if he cheats and throws it in your face and shows no sign of concern or care when you find out then he don't love you because when a man love you he protects you including your feelings. Ok, look at this we women cheat too but we are more careful we might cheat because there is something that our husband, baby-father are boyfriend are not fulfilling and we might step out of the box sometimes, but at the end of the day we will do everything to protect the man that hold us down especially if a good man."

"You listening Careen?" Kerry-Ann asks

"Yes I'm listening to you, Miss know it all" she said jokingly.

" If you have sex with someone else doesn't make you a bitch or a whore you have to do what you have to, to pleasure your self as well."

"It's so funny," Careen smiles as she exhales and share with her friends what she have on her mind " Charles and I relationship was good at first we use to had conversations about other things different from cars and businesses he would listen to my dreams and ideas and tell me how I can make them come true, now my thoughts and ideas are silent to his ears, my drams and goals are now invisible to him as well as Lacy and I, he buried his self in his work and care only for the amount of money that goes into his bank account on a daily basis."

" I know sis" Kerry-Ann said in a sad voice while Destiny wipe the tears from her friend eyes, "don't cry I'm sure god will soon send back your love or find you someone just as good" Destiny said.

"I'm sorry ladies but I have to run I have to go cook

something for my two men." Destiny got up at the same time as Kerry-Ann she have to reach home and get her daughter so Dwayne can get home before Kerry-Ann they hugged and kissed each other as they remembered that they were there to discuss weddings details. "Listen ladies we have to do this another time Kerry-Ann said as they blew kisses at each other and headed out the door. Destiny walked Careen to her car and reassured her not to worry, " everything will soon be okay sis" "thank you for being here for me Destiny without you and Kerry-Ann in my life I have no idea what would happen to me by now. Destiny holds her tight in her arms "you're welcome sis, go home and get some rest and stop the crying" Destiny said as she helps Careen in her car and watched her drove off.

# Chapter 15
## Put it on her:

"Hi Hon." Kerry-Ann said.

"What's up darlin' how was your girls' day out? Dwayne asked as he takes his hands and wrapped them around her waist. She smiled and welcomes him with a warm and tender kiss on his lips

"It was okay, not that we discussed anything about weddings it was more about relationships including you and I." He walked over to the kitchen sink, turned on the faucet and catches a glass of cold water Kerry-Ann walked up behind him and continued telling him what had happen on her girls' day out.

"It was mostly about you and I as I said before and Careen and Charles. Destiny is still holding back something. I never met or seen her with a man. The only man I know about was Handy and that was just a one night stand and even though she have a baby for him, and his name never left her lips not even once". Dwayne was uncomfortable he wanted to tell her that his daughter didn't belong to Handy she is a part of him and only him. He try to block out Kerry-Ann's words he couldn't stand to hear or even imagine Destiny with another man, even though she wanted nothing to do with him there is still a part of him that cares deeply for her and especially now that he's missing her touch and longing for her nakedness on top of him. He now know this was something more than just the sex with Destiny it's been nine years and he still cherishes every moment they had spend together, the first time they had met, he can still feel the passion blazed to life every time he remembered her moans the first time that he took her innocence. He tried his hardest to get back into the conversation with Kerry-Ann he turned around and his gaze met her eyes and he was blown away by the beauty that was staring back at him. He knows that he had to find a way to get over Destiny. He took a deep breath and followed Kerry-Ann into the bedroom; he sits on the edge of the bed and watched her get undressed.

"The only question that still lingers in my head is when Destiny asked me if I would break up with you if you cheated on me. I still wonder why she would ask me that?" Kerry-Ann said looking over at him, Dwayne's stomach rolled over as he waited for what might be the answer that she gives to Destiny. The silence was killing him so he asks her. "Would you break up with me if I cheated on you?"

She sat beside him and gazed into his eyes " It depends, for example if you had a one night stand or a long term relationship with someone else yes, and also if you cheat on me with one of my friends, which I know is not possible so that is one less thing to worry about" she said as she catches up her hair in a pony tail. He tried not to let it show on his face what he was feeling.

"I need a straight answer K what if I had a one night stand I need a yes or no answer," he said.

*I knew I shouldn't bring this shit up she said to herself I cannot let him know too much but how can I get out of this?* She said to her self. She took the remaining of her clothes off and began feasting aggressively on his mouth, he immediately turned into her and returned her kiss as he fought desperately to remove his clothes he became even harder as images of Destiny flashed across his mind. He knows it was wrong, but couldn't at that point help himself. He tightens his arms around her and rolls her over on her back; he grabs a hold of her breast and takes his time to make love to each of them. His mood changes again to being aggressive, finally tearing away his mouth from her breast and back to her lips he wrapped his fingers in her hair and pulls her neck back and bites roughly on her neck. He ignored the pain from her fingernails sinking deeply into his back as she moans and softly said,

"You're hurting me Dwayne." He remembered that it's Destiny but Kerry-Ann his heart wanted it to be Kerry-Ann but his mind was making him deliver only what Destiny needs and also what he likes wild and rough sex. For the first time he couldn't take the time out to give her the pleasure of oral sex that she loves so much, he was already too hard and couldn't wait to feel her walls gripped against his manhood without warning or teasing he pushed himself in her as she screamed out loud! He strokes her without ease or hesitation. He held her around her neck and asks the question again.

"Would you break up with me if I cheat on you? In pain she said no, he released her neck and rolled her on top of him.

"Fuck me baby!" he said, she tried her best to keep up but the mood that he's in it was no point even trying and what he wanted at that moment was not what they usually did and this frightened her while he held her waist and helped her move up and down on him faster. She was uncomfortable her man had turned into a stallion over night for years they been making love and she had never discovered this side of him before. She try to give him what he wanted as the tears fell down her face. Moments later he pulled her down on him and gets a hold of her lips again after he satisfy his needs, she rolled off him and lay beside him while they both tried to catch their breath.

"You ok sweetie?" A part of her wanted to yell noooo! but

she realized that she's a woman and throwing a tantrum is not going to help so she lied but intended to find out more about what had just happen.

"Yes, Dwayne I'm okay, but why did you fuck me the way you just did, as if you where somebody else or thinking about someone else?" He chooses to at least be partially honest with her and pulls her as close as he possible could toward him and purposely connects his eyes to hers. "Kerry-Ann I know that I hurt you and I'm sorry," his apology was soft and sincere, "It's just that sometimes I felt as if having wild sex is what I enjoy more I like that feeling of pleasure that it gives to me I won't do it again I promise". She lifts a brow and gaze at him. "So for all these years why it's now I'm finding out that you love having rough sex and who is it that you been experiencing it with for so long that you never had to try it with me before or even talk to me about it?"

"I thought it was something that you would never go for. You seem to enjoy me making love to you."

"I thought you only like making love to me; I thought you enjoy it as much as I do" She said. "I love making love to you baby, don't get me wrong, but sometimes I would like to try something wild as well" he said.

"Dwayne you shouldn't be walking around here assuming what I like, you should talk to me about it instead of surprising me like you just did. I'm not mad." She said calmly, "It was just a surprise as I said earlier, and I was wrong too and should have ask if there was something else that you would like to try instead of assuming that you only want to make love like we always do. This is a relationship that comes with compromising so don't ever feel like there is something that you would like to try that I wouldn't. I love you and will do anything to make you happy" she said.

"I love you too sweetheart and I promise I will share my dirty ideas with you from now on" she laughed out loud and kissed him and wrapped her arms around him. Even though

Dwayne had let her in and why his behavior was like that there was still something that was making her uneasy. Like the question he pretended he didn't hear who was it that he experience wild sex with and why he was so insisted on finding out if she would break up with him if he cheats on her and why he hadn't share with her what he prefers inside of the bedroom before. These questions travels around in her mind, as she lay there halfway asleep.

# Chapter 16
## I finally found him:

Destiny was frustrated by the sight of this man on line she was crocking up of the nerve of some of the men that has the audacity to send her an email. She's mentally drained from a long and hard day at work the last thing she needed to see were more muscles and cheap talk. She browsed through some of them to kill time, since the night was still early. She put her laptop aside and decided to make herself a cup of herbal tea as she tightens the strings of her silk blue robe and headed towards the kitchen. She returns minutes later and take her time searching through each Email hoping that she wouldn't miss a thing or anyone that made sense for change. She tried her best to keep it together from not breaking her laptop when one guy asked if she would give him the chance to let him sex her with his muscle. "One more muscle talk and I'm going to start screaming not one of these men are respectful enough or have the intelligence to send a lady a decent e-mail," as she murmured to herself some even asks for just the chance to taste her as well of the opportunity to give her the wildest pleasure of her life.

"I guess when men and women feel the need for sex all

they have to do is to visit one of these date site, because all these people talk about is sex or what they can do and wanted to do with each other." She said out loud and sucked in a deep breath feeling disappointed and now physically overwhelm. As she was about to hit the off button a message and picture caught her attention.

"*Hi baby girl,*" her stomach tightens as his words sinks in. She had always loved the name baby girl to her it meant something more than just being another woman the sound of it sounded sexy and sweet, she exhale and relaxed as she finished reading his message.

"*Your picture as well as your profile had caught my interest. Before I go any further I would like to say that you are the most beautiful woman I have ever laid eyes on and I would like to get the chance not only get to know you, but to spend my life with you. I really do apologize if my words scare you but I'm the type of man who likes to say what my hearts feel and if you responded back to me I would happily say that I'm blessed*". She was fascinated by his words it was too much to take in at once from a stranger, but as she thought about it she becomes settle in her comfort zone again. "Not only did this man pay me a complement and not only was he looking for a girlfriend but someone to settle down with to spend the rest of his life with. She decided to send him back a message.

"*Hi, I' don't know about spending my life with you yet, but maybe we can talk online sometime and get to know each other a little bit and thank you for the compliment.*" Before re-reading what she wrote she hit the send button and that was when she slapped herself on her forehead. "That was so stupid!" She said as she laughed at herself, "he might never respond back to me. Any way most of these men are married and just looking for a one night stand and that is something I don't want to go through again". She couldn't hold herself back any longer from checking out his profile and made it her duty to full screen all his photos not only was he fully dress in all of them but looked very sexy and handsome he seems to be the type that take pride in dressing he is six feet and three inches tall, athletic, non smoker owns his own car, a Scorpio and a partner at brothers law firm in Kingston. She could feel her nipples harden against her robe - she was instantly turn on even though she made a promise not to have sex with anyone else until she a least had an idea if he is single and he wanted more than a one night stand. She questioned herself - *why is someone this handsome, sexy, seems well educated and polite would be searching for a woman on-line.* But before she allowed her excitement to take over too much she wondered about the negative side - *what if he had ten kids of all with different mothers, what if he is a sex addict, drug addict or a alcoholic.* She kisses her teeth and pushed away her laptop and got up off the sofa to check on her daughter. She went in her room and turned the light off and kissed her good night. She was a sleep and did not want to wait around to wake her so she carefully closed her door on her way out and headed back to over to the sofa to turn off her laptop. The same stranger was on- line again he had send her message to add him to her contacts so they can chat. She quickly sign out of the date line and logged onto her e-mail and added him to her contacts she clicked on his name and she type and send "hi". *"Hi baby girl, how are you?* He asks. Her fingers nervously connect with the keys as she responded. *"I'm doing good, how about you?*

*"I'm doing okay I just got home about on hour ago from work took a long shower, poured a class of wine and decided to check my mail hoping you would be on- line or at lease responded to my message, and thank god not only did you respond but you're on-line"* he said she smile while she types. *"So you're telling me that you only come on line to look for me?"*

*"As untruth as it might sound the answer is yes, as I said in my message to you, you have drawn my interest.* "She tried to shake it off and turn the conversation. *"So what's your name and what is it that you do for a living?"* she asks

"*Name is Anthony Williams and I'm a lawyer a good friend and I open up our own law firm. Now I know you are just playing games with me because you already took your time to view my profile*" he said smartly.

"*Yes I did but I know a lot of people that put false information on here and sometimes they forget what their profile says and then tell you something different from what they had posted*" she said.

"*That is true but I'm a grown man and find no peace in lying to you, just like some people would say that they are a doctor when they're not*" he said.

"*If that goes for me I'm a doctor I own and work at D's Gynecology office in down town Kingston,*" she said.

"*Oh, I know where that is located*" he reply.

"*Really I never had you as one of my patients before.*"

"*I see not only you are smart, educated, and intelligent, you are also funny too.*" She laughed out loud.

"*When is your birthday baby girl?* "He is killing me with this baby girl shit." she said as she position herself on the sofa and sighed. "*October 28th.*"

"*Mine is October 24th,*" he said,

"*I know you're a Scorpio but I didn't know you birthday was this close to mines. So we can celebrate our birthdays together if you are still around,*" she said.

"Yes we will and I will still be around are you trying to get rid of me already?" He asks. "No, not yet you seem interested and I would like to get to know you some more, if that's okay with you?"

"I would like nothing more baby girl."

"I have a question for you." She took a moment are two to wonder what could he possible wanted to know about her being that it had only been twenty minutes into their conversation she was anxious to hear so she said sure.

"Why did you choose to become a gynecologist?" he asks. His question was plain and straight to the point she was surprise she had never met a man who asked her that question before. Neither did they take the time to find out the woman that she really is beneath her looks and the figure that comes with it. Not even Dwayne, who she had spend years with and also the mother of his daughter, but this man seems to be interested in more than just taking her to bed... "The main reason for choosing this career is pretty simple, I wanted to help women. Mostly the ones that are turned away because they don't have money to care for their health and mostly the women and young girls that are pregnant and can't even find the money to have on ultrasound. I'm not saying that I do it for free, but I charge half of what the system expected me to, as well as other doctors who believes that I'm taking away their patient and interfering with their prices because they had no choice but to cut down a bit on what their prices was or else they would eventually lose all their patient which is no concern of mines. I was blessed with parents who were able to put me through college and I was blessed with the knowledge and the capability to become a doctor so I put it to good use and help the unable. We are not only women, but as a Jamaican woman we need to set on example not only for our children but as well as others, so that they will one day believe that we can do anything we set our minds to as long as we work hard we can stay right here in our country and make it even better".

"Wow baby girl, I would never guess that is the reason. That's why I asked you so I would be able to know the type of woman you are before I ask you for your number."

"Is that a smart way of asking me for my number? I'm not going to even ask you if I fit into your category I'll just send you my number," she reply. "You fit just right baby girl and I'm sure I will as well," he said along with a smiley symbol, she ignores his comment and continued typing. "Anyway I bet most of your clients are high class right?" she asks.

"No, my clients are poor, not all but my interest is to speak for the ones that mumble and fight for the ones who are too tired and unable to move. "There are too many people that get taken advantage of because their education level is not where it should be for them to stand up for them self. Those are the people I open my office door to every day".

"I admire that about you. If more were like us this country would be so much better". Destiny yawns and looks at her watch it was 2:00 A.M in the morning. It's a great feeling that it's a Saturday and she didn't have to go into work but she had a lot of housework and other things to do. As much as how she enjoys the conversation with him she had to get some rest.

"I'm sorry Anthony but I'm so tired I will talk to you soon" He was disappointed but understand. "Ok but before you go can I have your number?" She laughs and sends it to him before she could say good-bye he was already sign off. She felt bad because she needed to say good night, she turn off her laptop and went to her bed room before she could settle in her phone begins to vibrate, she watched it almost fallen off the night stand before she reaches over to catch it. "Hello who's this calling me so late?" She said.

"Hi baby girl!"

Who is this?" she asks calmly?

"It's Anthony baby girl, mi just a call fi sah mi sorry fi sign out before you get the chance to say good night." He said. "Please! You did that on purpose to have a reason to call me," he laughs.

"I guess you're the type a girl that mi have to come to straight right? He asks

"Yes" She answers.

"Yes I did that so I would have a reason to call at this time of the night and I remembered you mention earlier that you're tired so mi a go mek this short. That wasn't the only reason I call. I needed to ask if you would have dinner with me later." *This man seems like someone that I would be able to have a long term relationship with so I have to play hard fi get if I want a long term relationship with him*, she said to her self. "I'm sorry Anthony but I'm busy later-on but this is what we can do we can chat on-line whenever I have time and when I get a day off again and some free time I might consider taking you up and that offer. Another thing before I go please don't call me unless I tell you that it's okay and if you have to call please call me at a appropriate hour because I have a daughter who spends most of her time sleeping and I work hard and need rest myself".

"Okay Destiny can I call you about 2:30 this evening" "how about you give me your number and I will call if I'm not busy."

"Sure baby girl" he said and gives her his number and she put it in her phone and told him good night he said good night and she hung up. She knew he was thinking that he has to step up his game a little bit if he's really looking for something more than just a sex partner and she feels good about herself for standing up as a lady for the first time in her life.

# Chapter 17
## Careen is tired:

"I can't believe this pussy- hole, after him drop a sleep pon mi pussy the other night him have the nerve fi tell mi sah him want some alone time so him a go away fi the weekend."

"Hello, Destiny yuh a hear mi?"

"Yes I was just thinking 'bout something" Destiny said.

"Who is it that is so important that my business for the first time don't mean anything to you?"

"I never say who I said something."

"Well the only thing that can come between friends is a dick, so who is it? Careen asks "Since you insisted on being in my business his name is Anthony and I met him on a web site."

"Just be careful cause nuff a dem men ya have a woman, baby mothers and a wife."

"I know I'm just getting to know him that's all."

"So you sah Charles a left fi the weekend?" Destiny asks.

" Yes" Careen answer calmly. " So why are you worrying about that? Good time fi you fi bring in a man."

"Destiny you never have nothing good to say. I'm a married woman."

"Cut the bull·shit, so what does that have to do with anything? Please don't accept that title if it wasn't given to you because Charles don't see you as his wife nor does he treat like one. You're way smarter than how you act Careen you just need fi crawl out of that good girl shale that you're in and start living you life fi you and Lacy you don't need Charles I'm still trying to figure out why you keep on taking what he dished out to you." Careen was listening to what Destiny was saying. She has wondered why she allowed herself to continue taking his shit. To her it was more out of respect than love as to why she stayed, but she know that he don't deserve her respect when he's not giving her any in return. "Careen you still there?" Destiny asks.

"Yes" Careen answered sadly.

"Stop depressing yourself I would love for us to go out to the club tonight but I'm going on a date with Anthony."

"Really where is he taking you?"

"I have no idea, because he don't know that we're going out."

"What you mean he don't know?"

" He asked me·earlier but I told him that I'm going to be busy so later I'm going to call him and tell him that I have some free time and if he's still interested he will drop what he had planned and take me out."

You use the keeper girl cards on him?" Careen asks through out her laughter. "Yes I did" Destiny reply proudly.

"Okay girl I wish you all the best."

"Thank you sis I know that you need some one to chat with right now but I have to go to the hair dresser."

"Pick mi up on your way I need some air."

"Okay that's a good idea you'll feel better once you're out of the house meet mi outside in on hour".

"Okay", then they both hung up. Careen pulled the phone onto the bed and kissed her teeth feeling unhappy and lonely. She lay on her back in bed staring the ceiling as she talks to the only one she feels can and will help her. "God I'm *not a Christian but I love and believed in you as if I was one, I have been a good wife to my husband, I obeyed my parents as well as my grandparents in all my life I wear the grown of a good girl I cared not only for the ones that I knew but also the unknown. I'm asking to please forgive me for any mistake that I make in the future but I'm a woman who need sex I reached my breaking point and don't know if I can hold out any longer my body craves for the touch of a man and if I have to break my vows and break the promises that I made I can only hope and prayed for your forgiveness.*

"Careen you home? Careen got up from off the bed and stood at the door making her self visible for Charles to see her.

"What is it Charles", she asked in frustration. "Why you inside here looking all depressed, you should be happy you living in one of the biggest house in Kingston, have the most expensive car park up in the drive way and an account over loaded with money."

"Listen to me Charles I'm sick and tired of you talking about cars, house and money those are not the things that make me happy material things don't make our marriage work nor does it pleasure me in the bed room." she said while watching him pulling out the drawers pulling out some clothes and carefully packing them into his suitcase to go away for the weekend. "Well I'm happy I don't see the reason why you're not," He said calmly.

"Oh so you're happy right?" she ask in disbelieve.

"Yes Careen my suggestion is that you find ways of making yourself feel the same." "I haven't been happy for years our sex life is fucked up; we never go anywhere together nor spend any quality time together anymore. What happened to us playing, hold each other and cuddle up every now and then. What happened to stories that you used to tell me and the way you used to tell me you loved me? Are you fucking someone else?" With one hand on her hip staring at him, she asked even though she wasn't sure if she wanted to hear the answer, without giving him time she continued her questions while she wiped the tears from her face and watched him packed. "I'm not attractive enough anymore is that the fucking problem!" She screamed and kicked his suitcase off the bed.

"Hold on Careen all these questions and accusations is too much for me to handle at once but to answer your first question - no I'm not cheating and no to all the rest of your questions now leave me alone so I can finish packing and get the fuck outta here." He said while picking up the clothes off the floor.

"You expect me to believe you Charles?"

"Look you ask me questions and I give you answers what you expect I don't give a shit."

"Don't fucking talk to me like that and I don't give a fuck if you are cheating because that little ass dick of yours and your lack of performance in bed I wouldn't be missing much".

"Careen I'm your husband and you will not talk to me like that". She crossed her arms and refused to take any more of his shit she knows that he will never change and she is done trying to change him.

"Yes Charles my husband not my father nor the God that I serve so in that case I will talk to you any way that I fucking please and since we are talking let's get something straight- that car I drive is my dead mother's land cruiser I traded and buy that one, this house that we live in half of my salary pays for this every month, and the bank account that is over loaded with money is also from my salary and some is my mother life insurance money. So next time when you feel the need to talk about what I have just keep in mind that I work hard for everything, not as if it was given to me by you as if I'm sitting around here playing a trophy wife. Remember that I hold my end down". She unfolded her arms and pushed her feet in her jeans and begins looking around for her keys.

"Where is this attitude coming from today? I might not

been the best man, but I have been a good husband to you."
She laughed as she continued getting dressed.

"If only these walls could talk Charles."

"I know that you're a independent and strong woman who
has your own way and firmly believe that you're the head of this
shit but the bible says." She looked at him like he was somebody
else. All the Sundays that I'd asked this mother fucker to come
to church and he always came up with some excuse that he had
to work or he was too tired and now he is standing here with
his hands on his hip quoting the Bible. "Wives submit to your
own husband, as to the lord for the husband is head of the wife
as Christ is the head of the church".

"Congratulations Charles," she gave him a round of
applause and walked over to him.

"But what you just said doesn't faze me you're so full of
yourself your attitude sickens me I don't know why I married
you there is not one quality about you that impresses me I
must say I was blind because now I truly see you and the bible
also says. 'Husband love your wives just as Christ also love the
church and gave himself for her'. I'm pretty sure you see that
right below what you just said to me, but you see what you
want to see. Just think about that the next time you decided
to throw scriptures from the bible at me". She grabbed her
handbag along with her keys and headed to the door.

"May I ask where're you going?"

"You can ask but that doesn't mean sah mi a go give
you an answer just like how you a go away fi the weekend to
where-ever and mi nuh ask you weh you a go, give me the same
respect and don't ask mi nuttin".

"Can't you speak better than that?"

She turns around and walks up to his face. "Yes Charles
I can speak better than this but I'm a Jamaican not English
the way how I speak doesn't affect my intelligence, this is our
language and I will be forever proud to speak it. A people like
you that make others feel like dem better than us because you

sell out, you look down pon you own because our language doesn't fit in your class but remember that Jamaica give you everything that you have - your education your degrees your businesses and a good job."

"I see you have an answer to everything."

"Good-bye Charles enjoy your weekend." He turned around and zipped up his suitcase as Careen walked out to Destiny who been waiting for her the last five minutes.

# Chapter 18
# He is the one:

Destiny is looking from side to side trying not to miss the restaurant that Anthony suggested they meet for dinner. She check her make-up in the rear view mirror every chance that she get... She pull over and decided to ask about the location of the restaurant even though she had an idea where she's going, but she's too anxious to meet this man and didn't want to keep him waiting, nor did she wanted to sweat out her hair that she spend most of the day at the hair dresser making sure it was done to her own perfection.

"Excuse me Miss, do you know where I can find Sweet Spot restaurant?"

"Yes, just continued on this road it is about four minutes down on your left hand side."

"Thank you so much."

"No problem mi love," the lady answered.

She pulls up in front of the restaurant and finds a parking spot right across from the restaurant.

She quickly checks her makeup again and inhales deeply even though she has no idea why she's this nervous. She tried to convince herself that this is just another date but instead of relaxing she could hear her heart beating out of her chest. Not even her first time having sex wasn't this nerve racking. She had managed to slide herself from behind the steering wheel and closed the car door. She pulls her black hipsters dress down and checked her nine inch heels to make sure nothing was on them. She crossed the street and entered the restaurant. Destiny looked around a couple of times before her eyes caught the most sexiest and handsome gentleman sitting at the bar area with his eyes glued to a Vibe Magazine and was sipping on a liquor of some sort. She knew it was him, but before she made her way over to him she took the time to look around at the colors they used to decorate restaurant and listen to the romantic music that was playing. She felt as if she walked into a whole different world until her gaze met Anthony's who was staring at her. She walked over to him so he would have a better chance of catching her if she fell, the sight of him was making her legs weak. "Destiny." he said in excitement.

"Hi Anthony" She extended her hand to shake his, he reached out for it and shook it gently.

"You look amazing baby girl," she gives him a cute and soft smile.

"Thank you, you look nice."

"Nice is good" He said with a shy smile. *Shit that didn't sound right* she said to herself but it was too late and in her eyes he seems to have a good sense of humor so she didn't worry too much about it. "Let's go up stairs I reserved a table up there for us."

"Okay after you." She said moving to the side so he could take the lead. "No we'll go up together side by side." He reached for her hand once again, only this time he held it as if it is was breakable. "God! Anthony up here is even more beautiful than down stairs." She said in amazement.

"I knew that you're a woman of class so I took the time to make sure they decorated it in a way that would go perfectly with your style".

The table was covered with a red, thin Indian fabric with silver hemming at the tail and three half white candles in the middle. Instead of chairs he used pillows. The menu is in a heart shape and he had his own waitress to serve them as well as a DJ to play whatever she wanted to listen to.

"What's all this Anthony?"

"I just wanted you to feel special tonight we only can get the opportunity of having one first date, even if every time after this feels like the first in reality this will always be our first date." She looked at him in amazement and refused to hide her blush. She took off her shoes tossed them a side and sat down on the pillow. Anthony did the same. After he poured her a class of Champaign and gazed into her eyes she felt he had been looking into her eyes for a lifetime. He asked her if she can dance and she laughed.

"If you call dancing in front of my mirror on a bored Saturday morning or dancing in the shower, then the answer is yes." He smiled at her answer and let it sink in before he made his move. "Well I can teach you if you like."

"Okay no problem." She searched his eyes for his next question. "Tell me something about you Destiny."

"What would you like to know?" She asks not sure why he's so curious. *I have two questions for you how big is your dick and how well can you use it?* She quickly changes her thoughts to something more appropriate before her questions left her lips and make its way to his ears. She took a deep breath and remembered that she is to act more polite and answer his questions in the way that she was thought to before she had met Dwayne that brought out the wild side of her. Tonight she needed to search deep down inside for the real Destiny the brilliant and intelligent one the one that she introduced to Anthony. "I'm sorry I ignore you for so long," she said as she exhale and relaxed her shoulders. "Well I have a daughter her name is Dasrine, I have two friends Careen who's a Teacher at the University of the West Indies and Kerry-Ann who works at Kingston Children's Hospital as a Pediatrician, these women are not only my friends we were born a couple months apart and grew up together, we're more like sisters. And my parents are moving back from Miami to live in St. Elizabeth. I don't party anymore all I do for fun is spend time with my daughter and hang out with my friends and when I get bored I go back to the country and vacation in my seven bed room house that I'd recently finish building. Anything else you would like to know just ask me because I might tell you things that you have no interest in wanting to know about" she said jokingly.

"Baby girl, in everything that you just said you tell me that you're family orientated, you like peace, it don't take a lot to make you happy, that your friends mean a lot to you and your daughter is the most important thing in her life because she headed your topic, only two more questions I have for you." She exhaled again and took the last sip of her Champaign.

"How old is your daughter and what happen to her father?"

*Why he have to ask me about the one person I was hoping not to discuss about tonight.* "Dasrine is going to turn ten next month and nothing happened to her father we decided to break off what we had". *I hope he doesn't ask why because the reason is none of his business at lease not now. What Dwayne and I had is our secret that we will have to take to our grave whether we like it are not, please god let him just let it go.* "Well ten is a nice age he said while skipping through his menu I have a ten year old son". Destiny looked disappointed wondering how long was he planning on keeping that information but relaxed when she remembered that it's only their first date.

"What's his name? She asked with a smile and interest. "Kelvin, his mother chooses that name she said she always loved that name I never got the chance to ask her why I just go with whatever it was that made her happy."

" It's a nice name," She said.

"Thank you" he said. They sit in silence while Destiny

thinks about why Anthony looked so sad as if he misses his son's mother something appeared uneasy about him as she watched his eyes became red and turns his attention to the window.

"So tell me something about you Anthony." She asked breaking the silence. He run his fingers back and forth through his tall hair as if he's searching for answers he lift a brow and realized the frown on his date face and knew that he had to snap out of his memories and make this date his top priority and give her a good time. He liked her a lot and it's up to him to get her to agree to have a second date with him. Maybe even having him as a boyfriend that would eventually turned to something else.

"First I want to say I'm sorry if I made you feel uncomfortable with my bad behavior by turning my attention to my memories. He smiled and gazed back into her eyes.

" I'm just a simple guy Destiny I don't have any secrets and I hate excitement and drama, but I love movies, music and I love to read - only love novels, I play soccer which is the only sport I'm good at, I work hard and when I do have some free time I hang out with my friend as well as my partner Troy at a bar where we drank a couple of beers and just talk about life and no I'm not a alcoholic." she laughed out loud.

"I didn't say that" She said through out her laughter.

"No but you're thinking about it when you walked in I was sitting at a bar and now I tell you that I hang out at the bar when I have some free time".

"I wasn't thinking that at all."

"So why you looked so disturb?" he asked sounding curious.

"Because you said Troy, he's the one that you own the law firm with?" Destiny become nervous and wondered if he's the same Troy that her friend is madly in love with the only man that once made her experience the sweet and wonderful feeling of being happy. "Yes, you know him?" he asked. "I don't think it's the same Troy Careen once shared a fairy tale of true love with but his name is also

Troy. I'm pretty sure it's not the same person." She said but still looked disturb. "Well Jamaica is very small it could be the same person because Troy also talks about a girl that he lost. He said it's the only girl he'd ever loved and because of that he refused to date anyone else he believed that he'll one day meet with her again."

" You know his last name?" he asked.

"No I don't but I can find out from Careen when I get home and let you know."

"Okay I'm going to mention her name to him and see if it's the same girl" "Thank you Anthony."

"Sure, I know what it feels like to lose the one that you love." Destiny notice the looked on his face again but this time she went ahead and asked him the question that was lingering on her mind since the first time she saw that look. "What's the problem Anthony?"

"Nothing baby girl." His first lie to her she left it as that and he continued on with his conversation.

"I feel as if I have known you for years Destiny, you laugh at my silly jokes you're a beautiful person not only on the outside you're ambitious, successful you're the type of girl I had been looking for. You would be a perfect wife." The word 'wife' made Destiny chokes on her drink.

"I see that you're not laughing any more did I say something wrong?" He asked looking confused.

"Yes, you did."

"What did I do?" He asked hoping he could fix it.

"You said nothing was the problem I know men and especially when they are lying I was in a long term relationship with someone that I gave my all to the only problem was that he give his all to my best friend I finally find the strength to break it off with him a couple of years ago and every men that I met after that makes me feel used and unappreciated they all lie to me at one point are another and gives me nothing but false promises. They wanted nothing more than just a couple nights of sex and after that I was just another girl. I'm looking for a long term relationship Anthony." She started to cry not sure why she told him that not sure if he wanted to stay after all that but she let him know what she's looking for in a relationship and it's up to him if he wanted to stay or not.

"Please stop crying Destiny." Anthony said as he reached over and wiped her tears away. "I'm so sorry for all you had been through but please don't let the treatment of these other men toward you make you give up on the chance of giving me a chance.

"Oh my god! I'm sorry for crying like this I feel so stupid." She said wiping her face and fixing her make-up.

"Don't ever apologize for expressing yourself and in my eyes you're way too beautiful to be crying and don't ever feel stupid because you're not."

"I'm going to tell you a story and after that I will join you and cry in your arms as well, but first I need to tell you some things about me I have to confess that I only had one baby mother I have been with only two women in my entire life, I'm not a woman beater I never hit a woman in my life I'm not a cheater I never did it before, I'm not a loafer or a broke pocket and no I'm not bisexual." She laughs out loud as he laughs along with her. "See, how I change your sadness to happiness as well as answer all the questions that you been yearning to ask me just because I'm a successful handsome black Jamaican single man."

"I must confess I was wondering some of those, but how did you know that?" I know how women think the first time that we spoke I knew that you probably said, 'god I wonder what's wrong with him?' and those where some of the other questions that crossed your mind as well". He took some of the pillows uses them to make a bed comfortable enough for the both of them as she stares at him for answer but instead he took her by her hand and asked her to lay down on his chest. She didn't hesitate because she had the feeling that he would never do anything to hurt her and she felt safe knowing that the DJ is still around playing music. "When you asked me what was the problem earlier and I said nothing, I lied and for that I want to apologize. I was unsure if it was necessary to tell you what I was thinking about, but after you tell me about you and your daughter's father I realize that it's a secret maybe one that you'd never shared with anyone else before, so I'm going to share not a secret but a story that has always been hard for me to talk about it's hard for me to bring back all those memories". Her attention was turned fully on him as she holds his hand and started playing with his fingers.

# Chapter 19
## I still miss her:

"Well it started on my twelfth birthday." He became tense so Destiny moved over closer to him to comfort him and shield him from any unwanted memories that might scare him.

"I was not excited at all my feelings puzzle me because at that age all I should wanted to do was to open my gifts and play with my friends and because I knew that my grandmother did everything that she could to made that day special for me and my parents send money from New York to assist with buying things for the party. I should've been grateful so I pretended to be happy and show my appreciation but still couldn't wait for everyone to leave my yard. So after mama got caught up with her church sisters talking about what people their age talk about church and salvation. I found myself under the coconut tree in my back yard and plopped down on a stone and buried my face in the palm of my hands; I had no idea why I was sad. I'm a humble person that fines peace in being by myself but something was wrong until this day I have no idea what it was. Minutes later I felt a top on my shoulder and I reluctantly lift my head up thinking it was my annoying friend from a cross the street, but I was surprised by the beauty that disturbed my concentration and put a hold on my thoughts. She had the softest voice mi ever heard. 'Why are you out here looking so sad for? This is your birthday you should be happy and stop with the long face' she said. Those were the first words that she had ever spoken to me. And I was happy they weren't the last. She sat down beside me looked in my eyes and repeated her question because my answer wasn't quick enough. 'Nuttin' man mi just tired that's all'

'You should be in there playing games with your friends'

'I don't play games. I don't have time for that.' I said to her.

'So what you have time far?'

'I read a lot and meditate'

'So you a Rasta?'

'Not only Rasta meditate'

'Welldem a lone mi always hear sah dem a hold a meditation' I had no choice but to laugh at her. 'So what do you meditate about?' She asks while I watched her cross her legs and moved closer to me. 'Things that I have no intention of sharing with yuh, why yuh tract mi down here yuh a police?' I ask her in a frustrated tone all I wanted to do was to be left alone I enjoyed her company earlier but then it was getting to a point where she was asking too many questions 'No she said looking sad'

'So what is it that you want'? I hesitated not knowing what to call her but she must have read my mind because she said Simone and caught me off guard.

'"What did you sah?' I asked.

'My name is Simone and no I'm not a police.'

'Nice to meet you Simone I'm Anthony.'

'Mi know that already'

'How you know that mi never see you around here before.'

'I just move here from Westmoreland I live two houses down the street from you but I mostly stay inside.'

'How old are you Simone?'

'Sixteen.' I had to repeat her answer twice because she didn't look a day older than eleven.

'You look like eleven' I said. She stopped talking and looks at me.

'I'm sorry if I offended you.'

'No man mi Kool.' I was more attracted to her attitude than her beautiful dark soft skin, her long Indian hair and her coke bottle shape she was about five feet and two inches in height she was very tiny but sexy. After that night we did everything together from cooking to bathing each other, I use to love combing her hair while she sits in front of the mirror and gazes back at me we never spoke of our age difference only in the streets people use to make fun of me all the time informing me that she was a big women fi mi it didn't matter to me at the time and she could care less what others had say until it started to get worse some of my friends stopped talking to me some sah she a go left me fi the first mature man that comes along with more money and a bigger dick. I must admit that their words got to me so I broke up with her thinking that I was doing her a favor by saving her from the gossip and the humiliation but the truth is I was concerned about me. I was tired of hearing my name in every conversation and I couldn't deal with the pressure of losing my friends. One week goes by and it was the most fucked-up I ever felt even though my friends and I are cool again, I'm back to playing cricket and football but I realized I was even more miserable even inna mi sleep mi a see her face mi couldn't eat, sleep not even school mi never wah fi go until one evening I decided to go to the only woman that I can talk to that will understand me. The timing was perfect because she was sitting on the veranda eating mangoes. I know she was well relaxed so I would get her honest opinion, she laughed when I told her my feelings toward Simone. 'Mi son these feelings that you're carrying is call love.' At that point I had no idea what she was talking about I thought love was only for big people and I was only twelve what could I possible know about it, as I began to fear my feelings, but she was right. 'Mi no know why you broke up with her fa in the first place.'

'But everybody a talk mama'

'Anthony people is going to talk you're not going to find everyone agree with the decision that you make but you have to do what makes you happy and fight for what you believe in remember sah misery loves company and those boys that you call friends that encourage you to leave Simone dem can't mek you happy and happiness is important, mi understand sah she's older than you, but what if it was the other way around you is sixteen and she's twelve then it wouldn't be a problem right?'

'No mama it would be perfect.'

'Nothing in life is perfect mi son, so go up there and apologize and hope to god she will forgive you.'

'Yes mama.' I put on my shoes and shirt and ran all the way to her house. 'Hello Ms Lawson is Simone here ma' am?' I ask trying to catch my breath. 'Yes man she inside dah comes inside.' My heart was pounding even though I had seen this girl a million times, spent so much time with her but the thought of seeing her face again made me nervous. Her mother wiped her hands on her dress and took two steps away from the wood fire while using her hand to fan away the smoke from her face she called for her 'Simone Anthony is out here waiting for you." A second later she came from her room with her hands crossed over her chest. I try my best not to move because I would definitely trip over her mouth.

'What is it Anthony? Mi a study hopefully to pass my exams with some high marks to get me into the twelve grade." I decided to get to the point before she changed her mind and went back to her room.

'Simone mi mek a mistake and mi really sorry I want you to be my girlfriend again.' She kisses her teeth and slammed her door. I felt as if my heart was caught in-between the door and broken into a million pieces. I knocked on the door as I told her that I love her the words that I had no idea what they meant or if it was really love but I knew that I felt something and if mama said it's love then it was.

'I love you Simone, yes I said it I'm in love with every pieces of you.'

I ran to the front door hoping I would get away before she opened the door I was afraid of her reaction to what I had just said to her and I didn't want to face her yet because I didn't think that I would had the guts to repeat it to her face, but the sound of the unlocking door made me wait to face her. The most she could have done is either laugh or tell me she loves me back. To my surprise she whispered, "I love you too." I ran over to her and scooped her up in my arms. Good thing I was way bigger than she was. From that day on we spend every free moment together more than before. I helped her study and she pass would all A's to move on to the twelve grade and I was doing well in school. Her final year in school was wonderful we were the perfect couple by the time her graduation rolled around I had saved enough money to buy her a bracelet that had pieces of heart hanging from it. We had to celebrate because she got accepted to the teachers college in Montego Bay, which she was excited and proud of. Both of our lives changed and everyone around who love us changes as well. It was late August School had almost opened for both of us we were playing cards under the coconut tree and drinking some lemonade that mama made for us. I was laughing and talking with my head in her lap I was so busy winning that I didn't realized that she wasn't laughing at my jokes any more and when I looked up to find her eyes connected to her breast with the most puzzled and unpleasant look on her face.

'Anthony my breast hurt, I think I need to go to the hospital.'

'Hospital baby, come on maybe they are just growing". At my age and being a man I didn't knew anything about a woman and the word hospital was a little extreme for a breast pain until she mention that she felt a lump so I call mama to call a taxi so we could get some medication and fix the problem at least I thought it would be that easy until we got to the hospital. After waiting for hours to see the doctor he call us all in his office so he could talk to us, at that point I wasn't worried until he said that he's not sure but he believe that Simone might have breast cancer. I was confused I thought doctors were trained to know everything. He informed us that Simone needed to do some tests to make sure. He gave us the name and address for a office in Montogo Bay that specialized in all different types of cancer. I still remember how the warm tears felt running down my face and even more when the doctor turned toward me and pat me on my shoulder and said 'it's okay son, your sister will be okay.' I pulled Simone in my arms and responded to his comment. 'She's not my sister she's my woman that will one day be my wife and in her womb she will carry my seed. Now move outta mi way.' Mama was shock by my attitude and so was I, but it only worsened as our problems grows. We arrived at the doctor's office about 10:A.M the next morning after explaining what she was there for he demands $14,000 before he would even look at her. All we had between Mama her mother and my school fees that my parents send for me to start school in a couple of weeks wasn't enough. I had to watch my grandmother and her mother get down and their knees and kiss the shoes of a man just for being two thousand dollars short for him to run a test. By then my strength was gone I was so angry I wasn't sure if my feelings were from seeing my grandmother stoop so low or it was from the reluctance of the doctor toward a patient or the thought of him trying to turn away a human being for two thousand dollars. 'Okay I will take it this time but mek it be the first and the last.' "Yes doctor.' they all said accept for me. All I needed was him to do the test so I could get the fuck out, because him presence made my stomach sick I made a vow to myself that

I would die before any child of mine see me beg like that. An hour later after the tests were done he called us into his office. It was the second time that I was called into a doctor's office only this time I was nervous I expected nothing but for him to say she was okay and that we could go home but instead he informed us that she had breast cancer in her right breast and he will have to remove the breast so it wouldn't spread. At that point I hated everyone around me I thought that it was everyone's fault as if the world was out to get me. I needed no friends or neighbors to tell me that everything was going to be okay. The last thing I needed was sympathy or pity. Daddy paid for her surgery with my promise to stay in school. I had to promise him but the truth is school was the last thing on my mind. I had to work to take care of Simone I had to some how provide for her and buy medication to help with her recovery. I was the man and I felt that it was my responsibility to step up and be there. I worked two jobs from cutting cane to clean floors and at Mr. Chin's grocery store. I paid for every doctor visit and school fees, during that time. I was eighteen it's so funny how age is not a issue anymore not even the doctors give it a second thought when I introduced myself as her man. Over the next four years I continued working my ass off. She finished teachers college and got job at May Pen high school. We were happy and for the first time in eight years my mind was settled since the doctors said that she was free from all cancer. We were happier than we had ever been and our love only grew more over the years. On my twenty second birthday she pampered me with massages to bathing and finishing with the best love making even though we had made love for the fifteen million times it felt as if was the first. She had asked me not to use any protection that time because she wants us to try and have a baby. I knew better than to argue with her and there was no reason why we couldn't, and somewhere along the way Kalvin was conceived. The first three months of her pregnancy was perfect not even morning sickness, and if

I never knew what it feels like to love a woman I knew when I first saw her looking back at her growing belly in the mirror while she fights to button her jeans now I know why they said only fools fall in love because I felt like a boy again. I was impatient overly excited and laughed for no reason every time I saw her face I got a feeling in my stomach I thought only women were supposed to feel that way. Everything was going fine until one morning I was in the kitchen making her some Callaloo and I gazed over to her sitting at the table and gave her a smile and she didn't smile back instead she frowned in pain. 'What is wrong honey?'

'Get the car I need to go to the doctor right now I'm not feeling good.' She mumbled. My heart was pounding as my feet became too heavy to carry me again feelings that I had prayed never to experience again was happening all over again I must have passed out somewhere along the way because all I remembered was me choking the fuck out of the Doctor when he informed us that Simone's cancer had returned only this time it had taken over her lungs, brain and her blood, he said that he is giving her five to six months to live, that I have to just pray that she hold on until she give birth to the baby. He said that she would stay in the hospital until she gave birth and that the total price is going to be one hundred and fifty thousand dollars and before he could admit her he needed half of the money. Mi rushes the pussy-hole again but this time him run, he showed no sign of sympathy all he cared about was money. 'Pull yourself together Anthony god must have a reason why he needs me back this soon.' She said gazing at me "Are you listening to yourself Simone there is no fucking god and if there is one what him could possibly want with you?'

'Don't question god's wish Anthony just be strong for me so I can be strong for our unborn baby and help me pray to god to keep me alive to give birth to this child.'

I was gazing out the window at the moving clouds that slowly turn dark all my years of living I had never noticed that before, but I had I reason to look to the sky as if I was really looking for the face of god who I was pretty sure wasn't real. But deep down inside I knew there had to be I just wish he could tell me why. 'We decided to check her into Lincoln Hospital so it would be easier for mama and her mother to go back and forth. I had to sell everything that was possible even my car and between both of our saving all we came up with was a hundred and twenty thousand still short of thirty thousand. I could work that in five months but I was also thinking about funeral expenses. It was the last thing I wanted to think about but I had to, she had no other family that I knew of except her mother. My father was the last person I needed to turn to because I didn't kept my promise to him, but it was my responsibility to take care of her. I worked morning, noon and night but the money wasn't adding up in time so I did the first thing that came to my mind and that was to break into a bank or a store bank would be too difficult as I thought about my plan the only place that I knew keeps that amount of money and would be easy to get into was the same Chinese store that I work for years. From the only man who offered me a job when no one else would give me a chance, but I had to numb my feelings of remorse because I would do anything for the woman that I loved. My plan went well and I was right he did have that much money. I was able to pay for her stay in the hospital and her funeral costs. I spend every moment that I had at the hospital to make myself useful; from combing her hair to painting her nails; to reading and singing to our baby. I even married her right there on the hospital bed when she was eight months pregnant. A month later our son was born with no complications. The baby was perfect we laughed and cried together for the last time. One hour after the baby was born she called me over to sat down beside her. She looked in my eyes, she squeezed my fingers and said 'Anthony I want to thank you for loving me, for being there for me even before we made our vows to each other you stood by my side through sickness and in health and definitely for richer or poorer. I'm in love with you with your beautiful soul, with your ambition, your knowledge, and your ability to fight like the man that you are. You are amazing baby and for that I will always love and be with you not even death can do us apart.' I was on my knees by then I couldn't find my voice to cry out I knew she was dying but I wasn't ready to accept it I needed more time with her, I needed her to spend more time with our son but she was ready. 'Please take care of our son.' I couldn't found words to say I will, instead I nodded yes. She thank mama and her mother for being there she kissed our son and then me as she closes her eyes slowly. I couldn't cry out I was in so much pain I moaned her death for weeks in the bosom of my grandmother arms. Which became the only place that I felt happy. It has been nine years Destiny and I still haven't gotten over her death." I don't know if his shirt was soaked from both of our tears but all I knew is that I never cried so hard in my entire life because I had no reason to Destiny said to her self.

"I'm so sorry Anthony no one should ever go through anything that terrifying I cannot erase your memories and even if I could I wouldn't want to because those are what you have left of her but I promise you that if you allowed me to I will help you find happiness again and help you through any unwanted painful memories that you're unable to carry on your own. I will bring joy and light to your life again." I said as I wiped the falling tears from his eyes.

"Thank you destiny for just listening I'm sorry if this date didn't turn out as you hoped," he said.

"No Anthony thank you for being honest and trusted me enough to be open with me and this is one of the best dates I've been on because of you I will now cherish every moment that I breathe." Minutes later they both left the restaurant together.

# Chapter 20
# The invite:

"Good morning Destiny how was your date last night?"

"It was amazing." She said over the phone to Kerry-Ann "I'll tell you more about it at church later, but for right now I have to go."

"Why are you running off the phone?" Kerry-Ann asks.

"Because I have some things to do before church and make sure you show up I need you to meet Anthony."

"Okay I'll see you later" Destiny said. Kerry-Ann walked over to the living room to look for Dwayne and not to her surprise he was passed out on the sofa half asleep. "Dwayne get up and do the dishes for me and I also need for you to come to church with me this morning Destiny have a man for a change and she want us to be there to meet him, so please get up -you just wake up and you a sleep again?" she asks shaking her head in disbelieve.

"Mi nuh go a church this morning, mi head a hot mi man," he said.

"Dwayne please get up you haven't been to church in months."

"Mi read mi bible and pray every day so there is no need

127

to go and socialize with a group of people that I cannot stand." She walked over toward him lift his head up and put it in her lap "Look Dewayne just do this for me Destiny want both of us there so we should be there for her out of respect."

"Why are you so determined for us to meet this man? He asked in an angry tone. "Because I never met any man that she had been with before and she's my best friend, if you don't want to come you don't have to," she said sadly.

"Okay Kerry-Ann." He got up and walked over to the kitchen to do the dishes as he begins to speak in his mind.

*I have no intention of wanting to meet no man of Destiny how can I pretend to be happy fi her because a part of me still needed her in my bed I never had a closure with her, I cannot help myself from day dreaming about the wonderful amazing sex that we had the sound of her moans still replay in my head at nights all of this I know is wrong but what can I do?* "Your clothes are ready baby he turned his attention to meet the smiling face of the woman he loved as he return a smile

"Thank you honey" he said sharply. "Mi soon done wash up dem plate here" he said nervously. "You would be done if you wasn't back here day dreaming." She said calmly, just hurry up."

"Okay baby." With that she walked away before he could get the chance to defend his self against her comments.

# Chapter 21
## Finally let go:

Destiny looking beautiful as always in a short skirt suit, a white blouse underneath a matching jacket, red pumps and matching accessories. Careen was wearing a fitted off the shoulder green dress and a open toe sliver sandals but Kerry-Ann was looking more elegant in a full white pants suit and a high heel black pumps.

"Hi ladies." Destiny said to her friends as they walked over to her with their man hanging from each of them arms. "Everyone this is Anthony." she said proudly with a huge smile on her face as she introduced him to each of them. In the middle of getting acquainted with each other Anthony stared nervously at Careen as if he's trying to put the pieces of her face together to see if it matches a picture that he had seen several times.

"I know you," he said huskily. She laughed,

"It's not impossible but weird I never been nowhere but from work to home and hang out with my friends once a week. I'm sorry but you have me mixed up with someone else." He put both hands in his pockets and stared even more.

"Forgive me for looking at you in such a unpleasant manner

but you look just like a woman in the pictures hanging in a frame at my friend house." Destiny interrupted "Oh I'm so sorry Careen I should've called you about this since last night about Anthony's friend and also his partner at his law firm his name is Troy".

"I'm pretty sure it's not the same person." Careen said in a sad tone let's just go inside service already started. She held her head down and took the lead before they get inside Destiny announced that there will be a dinner party at her house after church just among them to talk and socialize more with Anthony and his friend will join them later on. Every one enter the church excepted for Destiny and Dwayne "Dwayne let go mi hand, please don't upset mi this Sunday morning, I'm happy for the first time in years so please just let me go." Her feet struggled to stand as he pulled her across the church yard still she gained all the strength that she could and untwist her wrist from the palm of this hand "I will come with you Dwayne just stop pulling mi like mi a some sort of fucking animal, this is far enough what the fuck do you want? She asks firmly.

"So you really left mi fi a bold head."

She crossed her hands and looked at him puzzled. "Dwayne what we had is history and you a go leave mi alone before mi have to tell your wife to be about your childish ways that you're hesitant to put away."

"I know you won't risk losing your friendship over nights of endless passion of sweet love making."

"You're sick, you need help."

"Yes, you pussy a mad mi." He said gazing in her eyes, she exhale while uncrossing her hands and position each of them on each side of her hips "Look Dwayne we made a mistake and you're just having a problem getting over it mi move on, there is no turning back."

"But mi miss having sex with you D." he said.

"Exactly you miss the sex not me, you don't want me the

woman that you want and love is the one that you pulled up here with this morning hanging from your arms talking on laughing with each other maybe you should try talking to Kerry- Ann about your interest inside the bedroom she's a wild girl I'm pretty sure she will go for it."

He took two steps closer to her and grabbed a hold of her hand "But destiny..." she cut him off "Let mi go Dwayne mi have a man now and to me he is a keeper."

"Yuh don't even know this fool but yuh a come chat 'bout him a keeper just mek sure you keep him away from my daughter he shouted at her. "Your daughter who I cannot tell who's her father Dasrine and DJ played every day and we cannot tell them they are brother and sister because it would be too confusing to them everyone is hurting from our nights of just pleasure Dwayne you don't know what it feels like for a mother to hear her child ask who are where is her father and worse to lie to her. You come around her every day and she can't even call you dad." He could hear the hurt in her voice and for the first time he understands that he's being selfish and childish he never thinks about his daughter not being able to call him daddy. Destiny ignored the footsteps that she heard coming from behind her. "Are you okay Destiny?" It was Anthony she fell in love with the fact that he cared about her disappearance and he didn't just assume that she's okay he wanted to make sure. He had proven himself to also be a protector of the ones that he cared about. "Yes, I'm okay still gazing into Dwayne eyes he most have heard what her mind was saying because he walked away looking satisfied he get the point that she had no intention of sleeping with him anymore. She turned around and welcomed Anthony with a kiss on his lips "Thank you for making sure that I'm okay."

"You're welcome baby" he took her hand and walked her into the church.

# Chapter 22
# I prayed for this moment:

"Kerry-Ann I don't feel like going over to Destiny house to socialize with her man especially on a Sunday evening mi just wah go home, tek a shower, eat some food and relax."

"Dwayne we've already pulled up at the gate how would it look if we just drove away, I promise I will leave as soon as possible." Dwayne lay back in the front seat looking disturbed and over tired. "When you get with your friends dem everything stop." He kisses his teeth and placed one hand on his forehead.

"Okay Kerry- Ann I know this is important to you so this is what mi a go do mi will spend an hour and a half and pretend to be happy okay?"

"What's the point of coming if you're only going to pretend to be happy?" She grabbed her purse and slammed the car door before he could answer.

"When did you cook D?" Asked Careen while she opened up the covers of each pot on the stove and inhale deeply. "This morning before church" she said walking over to the kitchen "You wake up and cook so early something must change inna you life cause this is not you?" Careen said surprisingly, "Why didn't you call for help." She asked? "Thanks sis but I had help." Destiny said with a smile.

"Help from whom?"

"Anthony help mi when him wake up this morning."

"Wait a minute." Careen put the cover back on the pot and draws out a chair to sit on. "Okay let mi get this straight so mi no misunderstand what you're saying to mi, first Anthony sleep over here then get up inna the morning and help you cook?"

"Yes Careen." Destiny answered while turning her attention to look at the sky from the kitchen window but was frighten by the yelling of Careen calling out for Kerry-Ann. "what is it?" she asks as she come running "wha you call out mi name so fa Careen?" "Pull up a chair Destiny have story fi tell we but mek mi fill you in on where we reach, Anthony sleep over here last night and then get up this morning on help her cook."

"You fuck him"? Kerry – Ann ask firmly. Destiny pulled out the chair between the both of them and sighed. "No I didn't fuck him yet, we went out yesterday he spend most of his time talking about his ex-wife that passed away several years ago. After we left the restaurant he didn't feel like going home so I invite him over, he got up early this morning help mi cook then he went home." She explained to them try her best not to miss any details so it wouldn't be necessary for them to ask anymore question. "Now you two can stay outta mi business," she said. "You invite us inna yuh business we never have to know sah him sleep over here." Said Careen they all laughed as they took turns in pouring them self a glass of champagne. "Where are Dwayne and Anthony?" Asked Destiny "The last time I checked they went to meet Anthony friend I guess he's lost somewhere up the street" Kerry- Ann answered. "Careen." she said and then form her question correctly "Where is Charles?"

"Where he always been - at work she answer sadly."

"On a fucking Sunday? Careen you know as well as I do

that is fuckry you need to stop being in denial and start follow him everywhere he goes and try and catch him in the act so when you're ready fi divorce him you get everything fi all the years of putting up with his bullshit. Mek sure sah you walk away with everything wah him have." They all laughed again. Careen felt her heart pounding out of her chest as she heard men's voices walking toward the kitchen. One of the voices sounded familiar. A voice that she remembered hearing late at night when she couldn't sleep, a voice that she been missing for years that she prayed and hope she would hear again.

She listened to the footsteps as they move closer toward the kitchen.

"Hello ladies." Her heart stopped but it wasn't the voice she wanted to hear it was only Dwayne she watched him walked over to the refrigerator and grab the door pulling it open toward him as he reached one hand inside to pull out two Guinness and one Heineken that was when she realize there was a third man out there and it's a possibility it could be Troy because he drinks nothing but Heineken. "Ladies come out pon the veranda Anthony want all a yuh fi come meet Troy." They all get up in excitement except for Careen. "You okay Careen you want mi fi hold you up?" Destiny jokes, "Fuck off and no mi don't need your help mi Kool." She rolled her eyes and walk behind them for what seems to be the longest walk that she had ever done her heart skipped a beat and stop and started beating again only this time faster than before, as her eyes meet with the man that she has always been in love with she hold on to Kerry- Ann for stability. Anthony not realizing what was going on because he was so excited about his best friend meeting the woman that he believes can put back the pieces of his heart together so he can love again he walks over to them grinning from ear to ear. Ladies this is my friend and business partner Troy Scott, Troy this is the lady I been telling you about and her friends Careen and Kerry-Ann. They all were speechless but Destiny broke the silence and hugged him.

"Nice to see you again Troy." Without returning the hug tears rushes down his face as his gaze remained on Careen he pulled himself back and run down the steps with Anthony behind him. "My youth wait a minute." He stopped and wiped the tears from his face. "What kind of bomboclath games you a play with man who the fuck duh gal duh suppose to be?" He grabbed a hold of his friend and pushed him up against the car " because you see her pictures dem inna mi house and because you hear mi always a chat 'bout her you get somebody fi dress up and look like her fi fuck with mi head."

"Let mi go Troy listen to yuh self how mi a find somebody fi dress up and look like her all mi sah to you was that Destiny have a friend name Careen who's still in love with a brother name Troy and you insist fi wah meet her." They both were pulling their clothes together when Troy asked Anthony to walk back over the house with him "I'm sorry fi grab you up like that but yuh don't understand how much mi love this girl and even though you mention her name once are twice to me before she was the last person I was planning on seeing here today maybe because I convince my self that I'd never see her again." "I know what you're going through mi friend, you just have to take it one day at a time and god will see you through he had done it for me at lease your love have returned to you but my mind is gone forever" Anthony said to him. Careen remained on the veranda and watch as Troy walked up towards her. The sight of him made her shiver like none other had done before. *I didn't prepare for this moment,* she said to herself. Every step he takes closer toward her she takes one step back until she reached the open entrance toward the living room and made a run for it. "Careen wait a minute, baby why are you running away from me." She stopped and turned her attention to him from a distance "Maybe for the same reason why you run away from me this is not fucking real you're not here it's my mind, my fucking imagination playing with me again it happen to me before but it have to stop I can't live like this anymore." She screamed in frustration as he walks over to her. "No baby." He pled to her to believe him. "This is not a dream it's not our imagination I'm real and so are you I thought the same earlier but this is too clear to be unreal he reached out and put his hand around her and said "hi sexy she tilted her head back and looked into his eyes and smiled and said, "This is really you what have I done to deserve this moment again." He released her from his hands and led her over to the sofa. "Have a seat darling I have so much to say to you, so many questions I want to ask you I know it's not going to get done today but I want to start by saying that I prayed for this moment to come ever since you left mi back in the country."

"I prayed for this moment as well." She said sharply. "I missed you so much Troy." He reached over to kiss her but she turned her lips to the side welcome his kiss on her cheek, he held her hand and observed her fingers they looked the same to him except for the biggest ring he had ever seen on her finger. He cleared his throat and sat back in the sofa. "I'm not going to ask you how's life been treating because from the sight of you, you seems to be doing fine. I see that you're wearing a ring on expensive one at that. Are you happily married?" He asked. She had never lied to him before and fined it unnecessary to start now. "No but we're working toward making it better. I haven't been happy since the day I walked away from you." His expression turned from mystery to regret of being stubborn and didn't bother to look for her. He holds her and squeezed her as tight as he could. She relaxed and let him pamper her in his arms that felt much stronger than the last time he held her. He lifted her up placed her on his lap. She could feel the heat building up between them from the memory of feeling him inside her and how good he had felt. "Careen," he whispered in her ear she could feel his hot breath on her neck. "Why did you leave me?" He asks in a sexy voice "I was spoil and selfish," she whispered back trying not to change the mood.

"You weren't ready to change your life for me and I should

realized that the way how I see my future and how I wanted to live wasn't in the sight of your eyes back then. I didn't know what it meant to compromise, I was just mad because I needed you in college with me by my side in class, every day maybe even study teaching as well, but I was wrong Troy to try and push you into a life that I wanted and left you when you didn't see the same and for that I'm sorry. He could feel that her apology is sincere "You should've given me a chance Careen I didn't once give you any idea to believe that I had no intention of furthering my education. I thought you understood when I said I wasn't ready you had your life all figure out, you know exactly what you wanted and work toward it, I was different but I didn't had a clue what I wanted to do with my life but I knew it would be more than driving around and hanging out with friends. The only thing I was sure about then was the love that I had for you Careen this undying love that runs throughout my body like blood hurt more than anything I ever felt before." She looked him in his eyes and kissed his lips without saying a word she settled back down in his lap. "I hope you can forgive me," she said.

"It take me two years to find happiness within our memories I would be lying to you if I said I wasn't mad at you I was. I got a message from your grandparents that you was looking for me but I was so mad I just kiss my teeth and try to buried the times that we had shared, but as the years goes by and those memories rooted up and I find happiness and peace again even though you weren't in my life and I had no idea about your whereabouts, but a part of me knew that I'll have you again." Careen took the opportunity to glance over at his ring finger. *He's not wearing a ring that means he's not in any serious relationship* she said to herself. His looks have matured and his body Is well build, she remembered him taking his time to pleasure her with multiple orgasms, while he was on top of her stroking her with all the love that he had inside for her.

"Careen you okay?"

"Yes." She answered in a sexual erotic voice. Open your eyes sexy as he positions his face over hers' as she watch his face turns into a smile "What are you thinking about?" He asked curiously.

"Nothing." she said while laughing.

"You where thinking about fucking me or remembering me fucking you one or the other" He let her out of his arms and eased back in the sofa gazing into her eyes for reasons he couldn't figure out. "Why you so rude Troy I see that you haven't change much."

"Call it what you like but at least I think my thoughts out loud, you always kept yours inside only god can tell what kind of things been going through that mind of yours."

"Whatever Troy."

"Does your husband know that you have a fetish for orgasm?" "Troy I'm a married woman you cannot ask mi a question like that." "Okay I apologize that was out of line." He looked at her with a sad face. "Where do we go from here Careen?" She exhales and sighed. "Careen, Careen." It was Kerry-Ann shouting as she walks toward them in the living room "Weh the rass you call out mi name fa?" Careen asked still looking puzzle of what could be the problem. "Oh sorry." As she position herself on the arm of the sofa "Mi just wah fi mek sure sah you here mi because you all caught up in the arms of your lover who knows your mind probably on a island somewhere are just in the bed room" Kerry-Ann said jokingly. Careen kisses her teeth and looked at Kerry–Ann for an answer "Oh mi and Destiny want to talk with you because mi have to leave now, I'm sorry Troy but can we take her for a while I promise to return her." He laughed and said, "no problem mi nuh go nowhere just mek sure you bring her back" he eases back so Careen could have some room to get up, they smile at each other as she walk away with Kerry-Ann, they all pull out a chair and settle around the kitchen table once again.

"Kerry-Ann have to go so we are going to get to the point, are you going to ask Charles for a divorce now that your man come back inna you life?" Destiny asks.

"Jesus Christ you two couldn't wait till mi get home before you start to get inna mi business, and no I'm not going to ask Charles for a divorce because Troy accidentally show up inna mi life, the Troy that is sitting out there now is different from the one that I knew nine years ago for all I know he could have baby mothers in every parish here in Jamaica and women all over." She said angrily while slamming down the class of water on the table causing some to spill on the floor. "We can see that you're mad." Said Destiny. "But as your friend we can't tell you only what you want to hear, we have to tell you the truth you know as much as we do that Troy is madly in love with you, you shouldn't left him in the first place. "Shut up." Destiny said Careen "No I'm not going to shut up but you are going to listen." Destiny stared seriously into her eyes. "Troy did nothing but love you any fool could see that but the minute you found out sah him nuh go a college you left him with not even a good bye that was wrong and worse of all you carried and give birth to his child, find a next man and married him not only did you fuck up his heart but you stole away his chance of being a father so if him have baby mother all over Jamaica along with all sort of women I wouldn't blame him. We were blessed to have parents to steer us in the right direction, work hard so that we will have a better education give us a roof over our head and make sure we wouldn't know what it felt like to go to our bed at night without a good meal, not everyone have that Careen. Maybe Troy didn't or maybe he was just being a man taking longer to figure out what he wants. Now look at him not only a lawyer but also graduated top of his class. Anthony told me earlier." Careen watched her own tears drops on the kitchen table as she continued to listen to her friend "I bet you didn't tell him that Lacy belong to him" Destiny said.

"No." She mumbled "how long do you think you're planning on hiding it because Lacy looks just like him he sure as hell don't need a DNA test."

"I'm still married and I'm not going to divorce Charles." She said sadly.

"Let mi tell you something Careen. Charles don't want you, he don't love you, he don't respect you, he doesn't even care if you are dead or alive check her phone to see if he calls once."

"Fuck off Destiny I don't have to sit here and take this shit from you as if you're some sort of therapy this is my life and I'll live it in any fucking way that I choose." She pushes her chair back and ran out the back door while searching for her car keys in her handbag. Destiny and Kerry-Ann did not waste any time from running behind her yelling her name. She ignored them until she reached her car Destiny walked up to her and pulled her by her elbow hoping to get her to turn around which she did leaning her back against her car " leave mi alone." she said with tears in her eyes. "We're sorry Careen." Destiny said.

"If I said anything to hurt you or if I was out of line mi truly sorry but you have a good man inside dah and mi can't watch you turn him outta you life again." Careen exhaled as she made way to open up her car door. "Okay, Careen mi and Anthony is taking a vacation for the weekend in two weeks how about you and Troy come with us as well as Kerry-Ann and Dwayne this will give us time to relax with our men and work things out for us to talk about what is on our mind and hope to leave with some closure of what we want for the future" Destiny suggested.

"I will think about it." She said while sliding into the driver's seat. Destiny and Kerry-Ann watched her as she drove away.

# Chapter 23
## Careen:

*I can't believe that Destiny and Kerry- Ann have the damn nerve to come at mi like that as if I'm not capable of running my own life.* She said to herself while throwing her car key across the dining table. She wasted no time on getting undressed from the end of the stair case heading toward her bathroom but was interrupted from the sobbing sound coming from her daughter's room, she was frighten when she realizes that her door for the first time is closed and without knocking she pushed it open "lacy, why are you crying? And why you're not next-door where I left you? She kneeled down beside her at the side of the bed and waited anxiously for her answers, she stared at her mother with her swollen eyes and said, "My friend went out with her father I didn't want to go so I came over, that's not why I'm crying though mommy."

"Then what is it baby, I promise I will try my best to fix whatever is the problem" She wipes her face and looked deep into her mother's eyes "I'm not sure you can fix this one mommy."

"Try me baby" she said with confidence.'

"I need to see my real father I been thinking about him a

141

lot lately I just want to know who he is, I want to spend time with him and do things with him, whatever it is that daughters and fathers do together. I know Charles is here but he hasn't spoken to me I don't even know him. We never spend time together he never helps me with my home work, we never sits at the table and have dinner, he never asks me how my day was at school. Why does he hate me mommy what have I done to him?" Lacy had a lot of questions that brought tears to her mother eyes and it doesn't matter how much she thinks about it she will always be unable to find answers to those question.

"Listen to me Lacy Charles doesn't hate you, he's just going through a difficult time right now, I'm going to take you out more I think that's the problem you spend too much time at home" "No mommy." Lacy stood up looking down at her. "You always take me out what about our summer vacation to Miami with auntie Destiny and Dasrine you buy me the best of everything Mom but that doesn't fill the emptiness the space only my father can full, why can't I get to know my father?" She asked forcefully "Lacy get some sleep we will talk about this tomorrow I had a long day all I want to do is sleep I will talk to you tomorrow, I promise. She stood up and kissed her on her forehead. Lacy begin crying again and she crawled into bed and allowed her mother to tuck her in for the night.

Careen filled the tub with water and lay back as she let her mind drift back to the wonderful memories of Troy and regret again for the thousand times about leaving him. She reached over and picked up her phone from off the towel rack and press send to Kerry-Ann's home. "Hello." Kerry Ann said from the opposite end of the phone. Wah gwan Kerry -Ann?"

"Nothing just here almost asleep, you good?

"Yah man mi good mi just didda wonder if you can call Destiny and ask her fi get Troy number from Anthony fi mi, mi just no feel like deal with her right now,"

"No need fi that mi have him number right here. I figure you would need it eventually so I got it from him before I left

Destiny's earlier and I must tell you that I feel so bad because you left without even saying good bye."

"I know girl I was wrong for doing that but I honestly don't think I want to go back there with Troy."

"Why not Careen it's not like he hurt you before he should be the one saying that, I think you're afraid of allowing your self to be loved by him you're in such a fuck up relationship with Charles for so long you forget that the best and the sweetest feelings in the world is to love and be love by someone."

"I have to go Kerry- Ann I believe I just heard Charles coming up the stairs."

"Okay but before you go did you thought about the weekend vacation in St. Elizabeth we can bring the kids and leave them with their grandparents since they been complaining about not seeing their grandchildren and the kids can surly use a change of environment."

"Yes I can do that, but let me call you back." She hangs the phone up answering to Charles who's calling out for her while pushing his head in the bed- room to look for her. "I'm in here Charles", he walked over and pushed his head inside to look at her. "Take your clothes off and come joint me I have something for you." She said in a lustful tone, he took a step back and looked at her with a strange face as if he was confused by her question.

"Why you're looking at me like that was my question out of line?" she asked "Why you choose to nag me every time I step foot in this house Careen?"

"For all the years we been fucking you never mek mi cum, you never last more than five minutes and the last time we tried you fell asleep pon mi pussy you never take mi out, you never buy mi anything for birthdays, Christmas, valentine's day, you know how much I like concerts and they had one last Friday with all different female artists including my favorite and you didn't even bother to ask me if I wanted to go and you have the fucking nerve to ask why 'I'm nagging you'? What happen to when you use to love me or your plan was just to pretend that you love me during our first year of marriage hoping that I would stay and try to make it work?

"I love you Careen, I want to work things out." He walks over toward her and sits on the edge of the tub. " For all the years I been trying and asking you just to be a little more attentive to me and Lacy at lease try to treat me like I'm the woman you married to nine years ago and instead you act as if I was asking for the world now when I'm done trying you want to work things out. It's too late and you can keep everything the house, all the car dealers businesses, all your cars and your money I don't want anything from you."

"So you're willing to walk away from everything that we spend years working so hard to build, you're just going to walk away from them as if they meant nothing to you?" He breaks eye contact and said "I have a problem Careen" she quickly become curious to what her husband might have to say she reach for his face and turned his head to face her.

"What's the problem Charles?" His hesitation grew more until she ask again "I'm not attracted to you anymore he said with a uncomfortable look on his face, "don't get me wrong," he continued, "you're a beautiful woman inside and out I'm just not into you anymore." As he turned his gaze to the bedroom Careen stood up slowly in the tub with water and soap dripping from her naked body. The only difference in her looks is that her body is more toned her breast is still firm and her coke bottle shape is still perfect.

"What is it about me that you're not attracted to Charles?" He get up from the side of the tub and ordered her to put some clothes on. "I'm going to forget about what you just said to me because that's not the reason why you don't want to make love to me, whatever the problem is I have nothing to do with it." A couple minutes later she was finish in the bathroom and was looking in the mirror and getting dress when she caught Charles gaze glued to her naked body from his laying position on the bed. "Charles do you want us to go out for dinner since we haven't done that in years,"

"No baby let mi go pick up some food and we can cuddle up and watch a movie."

"Okay." She said. Within ten minutes Charles was out the door she couldn't help her self from watched him as he drove away from her bedroom window, what Charles had said to her earlier has now sank in and is now making her think of why he would said such a hurtful thing to her knowing that it's not true. She decided to take her friend's advice and fellow him. She pulled on a tight jeans, a T- shirt and a flip flap not even bother to brush her hair or look in the mirror after saying that she'll be back to Lacy she was out the door, but was stop by the ringing sound from her cell phone, she looked at the screen and the name that appeared give her a funny feeling in her stomach. "Hi Troy!"

"Wah gwan sexiness?"

"I was just heading out." She said with a smile.

"Are you coming over?" he asks. " Wishful thinking" she said throughout her grin. "It's not impossible." He said and then jumps right into ask her the question that made him call in the first place. "Would you like to have lunch with mi tomorrow? We have a lot to talk about since you ran away from mi earlier."

"I didn't run away from you I had some things I had to do and I apologize to you I should had inform you that I was leaving."

"Don't worry about it sexy, can I look forward to seeing you tomorrow?" "Let mi think about it and get back to you."

"Okay no pressure." They both talk for hours about what could have happened if they were still together. Careen glanced at her watch to look at the time and couldn't help but wonder where the hell Charles was she realizes that she was still sitting in her car in the drive-way. "Troy, can I call you back I have to go?"

"Okay call mi anytime." She hang up and pressed send to Charles cell phone. "Charles I thought you were just going to the restaurant that's only ten minutes away from the house and you been gone for almost three hours now." She said to him calmly over the phone "mi just left the fucking house Careen and yuh a call mi already if you must know I stop by the office and pick up some paper work." he said

"You know what Charles you puzzle mi, one minute you want to work things out and the next you gone back to being the man that I fell out of love with you know what do whatever the rass you want to do from now on you live your life and I'll live mines."

"Careen hold on baby." But she hangs up before she began to consider hearing what he had to say.

# Chapter 24
## First visit:

"Careen went back to her bed room and begin getting dress; she stood inside of her closet searching for something sexy to put on. She pulled off a bleached skinny jeans from the hanger along with a sleeveless black blouse and threw them across her huge king size bed, while she continued to pick out a shoes that would go perfect with what she choose she decided to go with a black open toe sandals that buckled up at her ankle. Her hair was already done just a few brushes and a little oil sheen check her makeup and she was out the door. Two minutes into her journey she reached over for her cell phone that was on the passenger seat and once again press send to Troy's cell phone.

"Hi baby, I need your address I'm coming to see you if that's okay." To her surprise she didn't get a response she glance down at her phone to make sure her cell phone didn't last signal and then she realize that he's taking the time out to think just like the Troy she remembered instead of saying anything she let him take time to think about her request. "Are you really coming over to my house?"

"Yes troy is it a bad time?"

"You must be crazy, bad time fi see yuh; you know how to

get to Stony Hill right?" he asked. "Yes I do, you know what just text mi the direction and I will see you inna few minutes." She said but once again didn't hear anything from him. "Are you their Troy?" she yells jokingly into the phone. "Yes man mi still dah here mi just drop off a the sofa but mi Kool."

"Yuh so stupid" she jokes at him "just text mi the directions."

"Okay sexy." They both hung up. An hour later Careen pulled up in his drive- way fixing her hair in the rear view mirror before walking up to his front door. He was on his verandah waiting for her arrival as he gazed forcefully at her double-checking to make sure her car was locked. She nervously walks up to him with a smile on her face. "Hi Troy."

"Hi to you, you look hot inna you skinny jeans and Rihanna hair cut."

"This is my hair cut Rihanna stole it from me." He laughed while leading her in to his house. "I see that you are still full of yourself." He said to her followed by an unexpected kiss on her lips only this time she didn't turn away instead she accepted it and return the favor of kissing him back. He walked her over to his sofa and helped her sit down comfortably.

" You still enjoy coconut rum and coke?" He asked staring deeply into her eyes as he sat down beside her. "Yes I do, thank you." She said turning away her gaze from his eyes to his decorated apartment she couldn't help but wander her eyes around his clean and well-decorated domain. She knew a lot about him but how well he kept a house was a unknown to her until now the soft fluffy carpet beneath her feet gave her a comfortable feeling of relaxation the lit scented red and gold candles gave the room a calm and peaceful feeling. He took notice of watching her eyes look around his apartment and was feeling good that her pictures was everywhere throughout his apartment. He walked over to her and handed her the drink and watched her as she put the glass up to her lips and took a sip and watched as it flow down her throat he never knew that watching a woman taking a drink of anything could ever be that sexy. "Why are you looking at me like that Troy?" she asks shyly.

"You know why I'm looking at you. My question is why are you here Careen? We talk about everything that we wanted to talk about at lease what I wanted to talk about, do you have something else you want to talk to me about?" Still staring in her eyes. She stood up and walked over to his window staring at nothing but the darkness from outside rubbing the back of her neck. "I don't know why I'm here Troy but I can leave if you want me to."

"You know I don't want you to go anywhere I'm just curious of why you would drove an hour in the night just to come see me, I was just wondering if everything is okay at your house?"

"Yes everything is fine." She lied to him. Something she wasn't planning on doing anytime soon. He walked up to her and wrapped his hands around her waist and whispered in her ear to come up stairs with him so he can show her his bedroom. Without hesitation she put down her purse on the sofa and followed him, before making it to his room he once again started kissing her and when she didn't refused he pushed his tongue deeper into her mouth making the kiss more hot and passionate they reached the room and he wasted no time and laying her down on her back on his bed pushing his hand under her blouse to get a hold of what his hands been missing for years. The dimmed fire that started the first time that she saw him again was now blazing throughout her entire body causing her to become wetter than the first time he touched her making love to her carefully and patiently. She definitely has what it takes to get him hard without much input. He manage to remove his hands from under her blouse reaching down to her pants attempting to unbutton them but she quickly remove her lips from his and asks him to stop. "What did you say"? He asks sounded frustrated, "I'm sorry Troy but I have to go

I shouldn't had came over here." She rushed to fix her breast in her bra. "I know you want this as much as I do Careen so why are you still putting up a resistance between what we are both yearning for."

"I'm a married woman Troy and I have no intention of cheating on my husband." "I can see that you are confuse and angry right now so I'm not even going to believe that fuckry that you just said, before you go look into my eyes and tell me that you are not in love with me and I promise I will leave you alone."

"Love is complicated Troy I just need to focus on resolving some things in my marriage right now just please understand." As she make her way down the stairs with him right behind her she walked over to the sofa picked up her purse and pulled out her keys. "Mi life is meaningless without you in it Careen, I love you so much what you expect mi fi do now? He asked sadly. She gazed at his expression and felt bad for him knowing that she felt the same way about him but she made a vow to her husband and I'm willing to stick by them.

"I love you too Troy more than you will ever know but the fact still remained that I'm still another man's wife I now belong to someone else." As the tears fill her eyes she was half way through the door and his grip was still firm on her hands. "I have to go baby please let me go."

"I can't Careen." She kissed him and pulled her hand away from him, "I need to get home to my daughter."

"You have a daughter?" His face brighten up with curiosity "She ran off the verandah realizing what she had just said to him that conversation was the last thing she wanted to have and it would be too much for Troy to handle in one night. Before Troy could reach over to her car she already started the engine and drove away. *Mi can't believe Careen is doing this to mi after she left mi fi no fucking reason she come over mi house, hot up mi head and left mi with a hard fucking cock. Not even cold water can bring this shit down and on top of that she left mi fi think about the possibility of that child being mines she get away this time but next will come around again.* He went inside his apartment and slammed the door behind him.

She suck in a deep breath as she pulled in her drive way.

"I know this is not right what I did to Troy I have to find a way to make it up to him god knows he doesn't deserve it. She got out of her car and checked to make sure it is locked and headed straight to the shower with no intention of getting dress she went to bed allowing the thoughts of what had happen or could have happen between Troy and her puts her into a deep sleep.

# Chapter 25
## I now see clearly:

Careen woke up and rubbed her eyes still half way into her sleep when she rolled over to cuddle with her husband the space where he should've been is empty, she turned her attention over to the clock that was standing on her bed side table to see what time it was. The clock read 2:00 A.M she become worried about her husband and searched desperately for a reason that would've kept him out at this time of morning. She rushed down stairs to his office to see if he was down there working on the paper work that he had pick up earlier but he was no where in sight she reached over to his phone and dialed his number she called three times and it when straight to voice mail her worry grew as she kept on calling but no answer until the sixth time trying he picked up sounding as if he was In a deep sleep. "Hello"

"Where are you Charles and don't play mi fi a fool and tell mi the office because you have no reason to be there at this time in the morning."

"Who is this?" He asked as if the voice is one that he had never heard before. "It's your wife, who the hell you expected it to be? The only place open at this time in the morning is club house and whore house which one are you up in?" she asked in a angry tone. "Okay Careen I will be home in fifteen minutes just go back to sleep" without saying anything she slammed the phone down in his ear, and ran back up stairs and sit on the edge of the bed watching the clock while she waits impatiently for him she listen to each foot step as he climbed the stairs by the time he reached the bed room she had already turned the light off and pretended to be a sleep. She watched him get undress and walk over to the bathroom not bothering to turn on the over head light in the bed room instead he use only the one over the sink in the bathroom. Soon as he finish and walk back in the bed room searching for his under pants in the draws she walk over to him and loosen her robe purposely watching it fall to her ankle she whispered in his ears. "I need some sex Charles, I really need to feel you inside me" she pled to him. "Go back to sleep Careen" he whispered back to her and turned his eyes away from her naked body.

"I wasn't sleeping, I was waiting for you and yuh still refuse fi answer my question."

"What question was that?"

"Where were you?" She asks again.

"I was just getting some advice from pastor about what can I do to keep my marriage, now if you will accuse me I have to leave out early in the morning you might want to put some clothes on before you catch cold." He walk pass her.

"It's like seventy degrees in here I don't think I will be catching any cold, and pastor must really be a man of god to get up out of his bed at this time to counsel you on how to keep your marriage, and I could've help with that I'm pretty sure I know more than poster." As she walked over to him and pushed him down on his back on the bed, she climbed on top of him and pushed her tongue into his mouth and captured his in the process. "Careen stop I don't have time for this, I'm really tired." He said while forcing to push her off of him.

"You don't have to do anything all you have to do is just lay there you know I'm the queen of riding it real good, you use to like it when I'm on top." She said with a desperate expression on her face. She climbed off him slowly and dropped down on her knees as she quickly grabbed a hold of his man hood without thinking about it she use her tongue on lick the head of it before she took it in her mouth inches at a time until it reached the back of her throat that causes her to gag, she ease up her head until the back of her throat is free. "What are you doing Careen?" she ignore his question and continued stroking him even harder than before. "Stop!" he yelled out at her, she still ignore him and continued, until he pulled her head from it and tilt her head back and hit her twice across her face without no remorse he watch her fall to the ground. She gazes at him and was puzzle by his reaction. "Charles you slap mi inna mi bloodclath face fi a suck you cock, what the fuck have I done, was I committing a fucking sin? She asked still looking confuse she knew that he didn't want to have sex but would at lease lay back and enjoy a couple minutes of oral sex, but she was wrong. "Mi feel like stab you inna rass fi put yuh hand pon mi but mi a go pray fi you 'cause you have some serious problems that need some serious help." She stood up slowly still holding onto the side of her face she become angrier as she looked at the marks that he left printed on the side of her face. Charles sat up on the edge of the bed looking even more shocked and disappointment by his reaction he throw his face in the palm of his hands and began to cry feeling ashamed of the man that he had become and hurt by a secret that he had to continue to protect, not only to protect his reputation but also of someone that he truly cared about. Careen rolled her eyes at him and didn't bother to get dressed she just washed her face and jumped in bed pulling the covers up to her neck and closed her eyes trying as hard as possible to fall asleep. Charles crawled into bed with her putting his hand around her pulling her close as he possible could toward him and apologized to her with a kiss on her cheek where he had hit her earlier. She tried but couldn't find the strength to push him away instead they both lay there listening to each other breathe at the same time wishing they could've read each other's minds, but they both knew it wasn't possible so they both drifted off to sleep.

# Chapter 26
# The unexpected:

"DJ can you clear the table for mommy and go get dress for school, I need to talk to your father?" Kerry-Ann said frowning over at Dwayne across from the opposite end of the dining table. Soon as her son finished clearing the breakfast plates and went outside she leaned over to him and asked him the question that makes him once again feel uncomfortable and now showed his nervousness. "Why did you pull Destiny to the back of the church yesterday?" She push out her mouth and cross her hands beneath her breast already knowing that he wasn't going to come out with an answer that made sense, but she felt the need to ask him anyway, hoping he would prove her wrong and tell the truth. Dwayne begins to laugh as if her question was meant to be a joke. "Why you always put shit pon man when dem nuh expected it." He said still laughing and not looking at her. "That still don't answer mi question I'm still waiting and mek sure sah you come up with a good story." He stopped laughing and fights to put on a serious face. "Mi no have to mek up no story mi just wah fi talk to her 'bout Anthony."

"What about Anthony?" she asked looking confused.

"Mi mek she no sah mi dah here fi her if him nuh treat her good are if she need anything." He said sounding unconvincing.

"So you turn security now or should I sah body guard if anyone should be concerned about Destiny it should be me or Careen not you."

"Fine Kerry-Ann mi sorry it won't happen again. May I be excuse please?" His question irritates her by the sarcasm in his tone.

"Mi no done talk to you yet, I want you to know that I feel it in my soul when you're lying to me and now is one of those time the reason why you pull my friend a side will come clear to me one day, you are my soul mate Dwayne that mean sah mi know you like a book as well as how mi can read you" She captures his gaze and keeps it steady until she was true with him. "Kerry-Ann why yuh a do this to mi now you ask mi a question and mi answer you, wah you want mi fi sah?"

"You give mi an answer that you think mi would feel comfortable with, just mek sure sah you nuh fuck around pon mi and tek mi fi fool in this community." Dwayne instantly felt badly about what he had done, the last thing he wanted to do is to hurt his fiancé but he knew that his mistake is not reversible he just have to try his best on keeping his secret secured from her. "You may go now." She roll her eyes at him, he slowly pulls out his chair hoping he would disappear before she thinks of something else to ask him. "And oh, don't even think about playing football today I need you to take DJ to school fi mi I have to go in to the office for a bit."

"I thought you were on vocation this week" he said.

"We're leaving Friday why take so many days off, I could go in to work until Thursday."

"But I closed up the store hoping we could spend some quality time this week. I didn't know that you have to go to work," he murmured with disappointment. "Okay Dwayne I'll take the week off if it makes you happy."

"Yes it would." He laughed and walked away.

# Chapter 27
# My true feelings:

Destiny was awoken by the rising of the warm morning sun penetrating through her bedroom curtain hitting against her face, along with a kiss on her lips from Anthony and his soft voice that whispered good morning in her ears. "I'm going to make some breakfast." "May I make you something as well?" he asked while pulling his T-shirt over his head?"

"Yes darling." She said turning over on her side preventing the sun from her eyes. She watched him as he left the room, she loved that Anthony had spent the whole night with her and not leaving when it was still dark out. She pushed the covers off and gets up to take a shower. Fifteen minutes later she was searching for a dress, She pulled out a long white summer dress and decided to put that on after rubbing on moon light path one of her favorite scents from Bath and Body. She brushed her hair and watched it falls and lays on her shoulders. After putting on some lip-gloss she walked out of the room and headed toward the kitchen. A plate with fried plantain and eggs with two slices of buttered bread was sitting on her end of the table along with some freshly cut yellow roses from her backyard and a note that read. *I couldn't found any that is as beautiful as you.* She smiled and remained in silence so he wouldn't move from the position that he was in. She stole the moment to admire him from the back, while he uses a bit of his muscle to flip and turn the eggs. As he turns around to reach for a plate from the cupboard the beauty that is sitting at the table captivated him and brought his thought to something more than just fixing her breakfast. "Oh, wah gwaan baby girl, mi never heard you come in." "Because I was very quiet, on propose." she added with a lustful expression on her face. "How long you been there?" he ask turning his attention back to the pot on the stove. "Long enough to use my mind and get you undressed, make love to you and watch your juice flow from the tip of your penis".

"You sah something baby girl?" he ask while putting his egg on his plate.

"Oh I was just saying that I arrived a couple of minutes ago." She said putting her hands against her forehead as she felt disgusted by her own thoughts. "Can you come here for a minute Anthony I have something to tell you?" Pushing her plate to the side.

"Mi a come baby girl let mi turn this stove off." She waits patiently using that time to come up with a good reason for not doing what she is about to do, but was unsuccessful by the time he came rushing over to her, "You Kool?" he asked leaning down on the table. "No, I need you." She mumbled before he could ask again her tongue was already in his mouth. He pulled back just enough to ask "Are you sure you want to do this?"

"Yes I'm sure if you want to?" Without answering her question he lifted her up and put her on the table slowly pushing his hands under her dress pulling down her panties and tosses it on the floor. Her body felt tight and incredibly feminine against his body, he lifted her more into his arms, still kissing her. She placed one foot on his shoulder and spread the other one as far as it could go giving him access to enter her.

He pushed his manhood slowly inside her and pumped deeply as he watched her close her eyes and listen to the sounds of her moans, minutes later he said the words that Destiny wasn't expecting to hear at that moment those three little words that she still don't have a clue what they meant are if they're really real. "I love you." she removed her foot from his shoulder and wrapped it around his waist pulling him down more on her, he gazed into her eyes while he used one hand tilting her ass up on him as he pushed deeper and harder inside of her. This time she holds his gaze for the longest time and only let her lips move. "I love you too baby." He pulled her breasts out and began caressing them one at a time until he ripped her dress off completely and flipped her over on her stomach instructing her to push her ass up so that he could make love to her in one of her favorite positions. After almost half an hour of doggy style she turned over and sat slowly and then jump down off the table she pushed him up against the it and instructed him to lay on his back she climbed on top of him, and took control and reached for his ten inches and sat down slowly on it riding it in a way that had his toes curled under and his eyes roll over reminding her of the movie *The Exorcism of Emily Rose*, he hold on tight to her breast pulling it down to his mouth to prevented him from screaming like a child when she tightens her pussy against the nakedness of his dick as she moves up and down in slow motion. A couple of minutes later they both cum and she made an attempt to roll off him but he stopped her and held her in his arms, complementing her on a job well done. Still holding her, running his fingers one at a time down her spine he said "I meant what I said earlier, I really do love you, you mek mi feel complete again and fi that I want to say thank you." She lifted her head up and sat up straight. "And I really do love you too baby, you're the first man that ever mek mi feel this happy, so safe and so needed." She said thinking about what she had just said the truth is she really was only sure about him making her feel safe and needed but the part about she loving him back was still unsure to her.

"You're so incredible, sexy, and beautiful baby girl, ever since the death of Simone I never knew that there is another woman alive out there that could ever make mi feel like this and I can promise you this right now that, if you give mi a chance fi be that only man inna life mi wee live the rest of mi life making sure that you're happy in every way possible, all mi want is fi you fi love mi the same and respect mi as much as I respect you." Tears ran down her cheeks as he pulled her down toward his strong muscular body holding her tight in his arms, she couldn't find words at the moment. Instead she turned her attention to his rising manhood that put her in the mood for round two. He lifted her up this time and took control they made love for hours then they both showered and he fell a sleep while she lay next to him with nothing on her mind except for what Anthony had told her earlier while she tries to figure out what it is that she feels for him if anything at all.

# Chapter 28
## Girls' talk:

"Good morning Careen." Destiny said from the other end of the phone sounding jolly than normal. "Wah gwam mi gal? Careen asks sounding sad and bored.

"How you sound so tired at this time inna the morning, Charles finally give you some?"

"I wish, mi just done running eight miles on the tread mill and was 'about to do some sit-ups." Answering her friend's question as she sits down on her sofa.

"Why are you running eight miles? You training fi the Olympics or something that I don't know about." She asked.

"No but Charles sah mi no look attractive to him so mi a work out." Destiny immediately became upset, "why you mek that husband of yours a turn you inna fool Careen."

"And some way along the line him slap mi inna mi face fi give him oral sex are mek and attempt I should say." Destiny was choking on her orange juice that she's sipping on before breakfast from her laugher that she fights desperately to hold back out of respect but instead it comes out harder and louder. "Wah the fuck so funny Destiny? this is why mi can't tell you anything, because everything is a good joke to you."

"I'm sorry Careen, but mi a try fi understand what would mek a man slap him wife inna her face fi a give him oral sex".

"I have no idea," said Careen while Destiny went back to laughing and coughing. "Destiny switch over and call Kerry-Ann 'because mi can't stand your ass laughing inna mi ears" Careen said. Tired of hearing Destiny laugh hoping that Kerry-Ann would be more understanding. "What is it?" Kerry-Ann picked up the phone and answered in an upset tone. Destiny intentionally ignored her question and continued laughing. "Hi Kerry-Ann." Careen said.

"What is wrong with Destiny why is she laughing so hard?" asked Kerry Ann.

"Mi just tell her something and the fool tek it fi joke, this is why I don't like telling her anything because she still behave like a fucking child."

"Calm down Careen, what is it that you told her?"

"Nothing I don't want to talk about it again."

"Charles slap her inna her face because she tries to give him oral sex." Destiny said trying to stop her laughing long enough to get the words out.

"Destiny come off a this bloodclath with all that laughing mek mi talk to Careen". "No mi wah hear this, Careen sorry fi laughing but it's really funny, but I promise I can keep it together, okay?" she said in a soft voice. They both pretended as if she wasn't on the other line while Kerry-Ann helped her friend to understand the reason for Charles behavior.

"Careen I know this is going to hurt like crazy sis, but it's something we had told you before and deep down I believe you know it's true, but Charles doesn't want you." Kerry-Ann said, feeling her friend's pain along with her as she listened to Careen sob. "Does Charles ever talk about any of his past relationships? Careen sighed and answered, "No."

"Charles is gay sis, I'm sorry to be the one to tell you this but based on what I have seen and what you share with me I'm ninety five percent sure that he is"

"No Kerry-Ann it's not possible he's married to me, I'm his wife" Careen screamed out in anger and pain trying to convince her friends or maybe herself that he's not. "He only married you to use you as a cover up, how would it look in the eyes of others that he's gay and to his friends, he is a business man Careen, do you think that his businesses would be this successful if people found out that he's the biggest batty-man in Kingston?" Careen hesitated before answering her friend question. "No he wouldn't."

"And not only that but he would be putting his life at risk and lose all his respect, so when he first met you and asked you to be his wife he knew exactly what he was doing. He was planning on using you and is still using you Careen". "I'm still not buying it Kerry-Ann. Charles loves me and I love him, he's just going through some things right now." Careen said sounding defensive.

"Okay then since mi a you friend and friends help each other mek mi help you understand, the only time you remember fucking him was during your first year of your marriage, which only lasted couple minutes you never cum and him never give a fuck if you did or not, everything that you two did together was during the first year, the reason for that is because he was trapping you into falling in love with him knowing that if you do you will not easily give up and leave him. Him mek you believe sah he's in love with you by buying the house and being there for you during your last stage of pregnancy and help care for Lacy, back than no one could tell mi sah him never love you and that everything was all a plan, don't get mi wrong Careen maybe he did try to love you as a husband he's supposed to love his wife, but if you only have interest in men then it's not possible, for a woman that is so strong, so beautiful and sexy and still you can't give your husband a hard- on something has to be wrong somewhere and if he was cheating on you with a woman his behavior would be different he would at least come home and make love to you every once in a while. Hello!" Kerry-Ann said loudly after waiting minutes without any response from Careen, she was surprised and disappointed that the friend that responded back to her wasn't the one that she wanted to hear from at that point. "Destiny did Careen hang up?" kerry-Ann asks.

"I guess she did and I agreed with you Kerry-Ann I believe that he's gay and just using her but how do we get Careen to believe this shit?" " She will but it's going to take time she's a bright girl and it's not everyday someone tells a woman that her husband is gay, especially when she put her all into that marriage working overtime to make it work, we just have to make sure that she come on our weekend get away with us." Kerry-Ann said.

"She will sis, I'm just worried about her maybe we should go over there."

"No D she needs some time to think, any way mi a go finish mek some food fi Dwayne so mi wee chat to you later."

"Okay Kool." They both hang up.

# Chapter 29
# I have to find happiness
# within myself:

Careen sat down at her dining room table, thinking about the shit that her friends had revealed to her about her husband. Even though what her friends said hurts, what hurt her the most is that it's true she now knows that she cannot allow herself and her daughter to continued getting hurt and after hours of thinking she made up her mind that she had to make herself happy again. She searches through her phone to call someone that has always been there for her in any decision that she had to make he had always listen and gives good advice.

"Hello, this is Mrs. Spencer how may I help you? The voice and the other end made Careen unsure of what to say and the faces of her parents' flashes in front of her eyes. If they were around this phone call wouldn't be necessary.

"Good evening ma'ma she said in a shallow tone, is pastor home?"

"No mi dear him just steps out is there something that I can help you with?" Careen hesitated a part of her felt the need to talk to her woman to woman but the other felt as if she wouldn't be much help even though she has always been sweet to her and even babysat Lacy a couple of times when she was much smaller. There is still something unsettling about inviting her in to her business. "I'm just going through some personal problems and I need a word of advice before I make my final decision, so maybe you can have him call me as soon as he gets home." Careen said about to hang up the phone when Mrs. Spencer asks the question  that she hoped she wouldn't. "What is wrong Careen maybe the old lady here can help," she said making her self-comfortable on the edge of her bed. "It is nothing serious ma'ma just that I'm going to file for a divorce and I needed pastor's input since he was the one that married us in the first place and give us years of counseling, I just feel the need out of respect to let him know I have to end it now". Careen knew that she had made up her mind regardless of what he might say but still had to show respect.

"A divorce! She shouted in surprise, and you call that nothing Careen what happened between you and Charles now, him a beat you? Him have other woman outta street?"

"Wah mi go tell this woman mi business fa," she mumbles to herself. She allows her questions to linger in her head as she tries to find the safest answer to each of them. "He slapped me in my face once, and I'm sure he's cheating." She tries to keep her answers simple, but enough to keep her from not asking anything else. The last thing she wanted to do is discuss her sex life with her. "Careen stop beating around the bush and talk to mi so mi can understand why you want to divorce your husband after all these years" *god why she have to go there*? She asks her self. "We're having problems in the bed room, he haven't made love to me for years now and when I touch him he walks away and demands me to stop. It's got to the point now that he can't even get his dick hard for me anymore". Careen waited patiently for her respond and was ready for whatever she had to say so she could get the hell off the phone and go to bed. "Careen, what I'm about to sah to you I haven't said to anyone I never talk about it to no one except god and myself not even to mi daughter, but I'm going to share it with you and I expect you to keep it to yourself, you hear me?" She confirmed that Careen would respect her request. "Yes ma'ma she said in a tone that sound convincing enough allowing her to continue with what she have to say. "I'm forty seven years old and it's been ten years now since my husband has not had sex with me, at first I thought it was me, like us women always quick to believe that we're the problem, so I Did everything to made it better I was obedient to everything that he ask of me without no questions and I never complained. I start going to the gym more I get my hair and nails done-everything, I wear nothing but what was in style from my nightgown down to mi underwear but nothing changes and eventually I grew tired of trying, until one night we were sitting at the dinner table and I decided to ask him what was his problem because obviously I wasn't, so it had to be him or something that had to do with him. His answer was clear and sudden; he said that his father used to sexually abuse him until he was age ten and ever since there's a part of him that is attracted to men. Until ten years ago he realized that his desire grows more for men he said he can no longer lie to himself and will not have intercourse with men and I at the same time so he choose to stick to men. He was honest Careen, he said if I wanted to leave he would understand but I could no longer fulfill his needs. But I stayed and I prayed for months at first for god to change him and give me back my husband and forgive him not for a sin that he had brought up on himself but for the sin that was brought up on him. And then I prayed for myself to be happy to find peace within myself and I did. I found happiness within the church, my surroundings and my daughter. Pastor and I take vacation twice a year we talk and listen to each other we help those who need it and those who are incapable of asking for it. My point to this story is that don't tell pastor anything only god can judge you he is the only one you need to talk to in times like this and if you listen you will hear what he have to say. You cannot change Charles, love yourself and take care of you before you can do it for anyone else, find whatever and who ever makes you happy and stay with him are it. You're a beautiful young girl Careen you have no reason to turn your life over to Charles go out there and find that whatever it is that is missing from your life." This was more than what Careen was hoping to hear everything that Mrs. Spencer said was true and her words and advice Careen took with her through every decision that she made from then on.

"Careen you there?"

"Yes ma'am," she said between her sobs.

"Mi hope you listen to what mi just sah to you, mi have to go now so mi will talk to you later."

"Yes ma'am." As Careen hung up the phone she couldn't help but think about pastor what he had been through with his father and the man that he had become today. She wiped her face while making her way up to her bath- room. She sits in the tub of warm water everything that she had been through and still going through make her realize for the first time that Charles doesn't love her and never did. She had worked for years trying to turn their house into a home and filled with love and happiness for them to have the type of marriage her parents had but if it wasn't meant to be then it simple weren't meant to be.

# Chapter 30
# I'm still in love with you:

Hours had passed by and no sign or a phone call from Charles. I glanced at my clock and it was 7:30 P.M. I needed to clear my head; I needed someone to hold me and assured me that everything is going to be okay. And the only person who can do this for me is Troy. I jumped out of bed and started running through my closet looking for something to wear. *I have to go and see him* she said to her self. Careen reached for her phone to call his house to let him know that she's coming over, but decided against it instead she thought it would a good idea to surprise him. Troy was home cooking and listening to music when he heard a knock on his door, he wiped his hands on the dish towel and made his way over to the door already with the words in his head of what he wanted to say to Anthony when he opened the door, but it wasn't who he expected and he couldn't find the words that he wanted to say to Careen who's standing at his front door.

"What is it Careen, or should I say how may I help you?" She quickly forgave his rudeness and understood his reason for it. She brushed pass him and made her way over to the kitchen and poured herself a glass of water. He closed the door and walked toward her pulling out a chair and sat down unable to remove his eyes from her. "Mi sure sah you no come over here fi water, the last you come over here inna skinny jeans and Rihanna hair style turn mi on and left mi with a hard dick. Now you come inna long, hair short dress and heels." He stands up and walks over to her wrapped his hands around her neck and pulled her close to him. "Why are you afraid of me Careen?" "I'm not afraid of you." She said pushing him away enough to get away from him she fetched her keys from her purse making her way to the front door. But he get a hold of her wrist swinging her around to face him pushing her against the door carefully and begin to kiss her she didn't refuse but give back one of the most sexiest kiss that she had yet to give to anyone else. She releases his tongue soon as she felt his manhood rises and pressed against her belly "I have to go Troy I can't do this." "Then why are you breathing so hard?" He whispered purposely allowing his mouth to move up and down against her ear. "I'm not breathing hard." She tries to untwist her hand from his. "Yes, you are and the only reason why you're here is because you want me to make love to you so stop trying to play games and relax so I can give you what you been longing for."

"No Troy, just stop." She pushed him away and ran up to his bedroom. He let her go, and ignored the urge to run after her. He returned to the kitchen, fixed her a plate and brought it up to her. He slowly walked up behind her and touches her lightly on her shoulder trying not to frighten her. She turned around removing her gaze from the beautiful moon- light that was shining directly into the room giving it a calm blue scene and a peaceful feeling she turned around and gazed in his eyes in that vary moment her whole history with Troy replay in her mind there is no way on earth she could convinced her self that she doesn't need him as badly as how he needed her, she's addicted to him more now than before. "I brought you some food." He handed her the plate turning his head to the side she noticed the sad expression on his face and heard it in his voice. "Thank you." She said watching him take a seat on his bed. He fell back and begin staring at the happy images of her in the pictures that's hanging from the wall. He was deep and last in his memories that he didn't realized that she's making her way over to him he was frighten by her voice when she asked him if he was okay. "Yes mi good man, you leaving now?" he asks.

"No." She said instead she slowly climbed on top of him lowering her face to his and begin kissing him, he was surprised and wasn't sure if he wanted her to do it are not. The last thing he needed was for her to leave him with another hard-on but he relaxed and accepted her kiss she lifted her head up while removing her hair from his face and reassured him how much she loved and misses him.

"I want you to know that I never stop loving you Troy I keep every memory of us alive in my heart. You are the only man that I ever truly loved." "I know that you love me Careen I never thought twice about that, I spent each day cherishing each and every one of your smiles that I held as a prisoner in my memories, everything about you the way you stand in front of the mirror while you're getting dress, the way you move her hands when you talk, the way how you sits and cross your leg with such style, the look on your face when you're asleep and the expression that you give when you are upset all of these things that you do make me love you more each day". He didn't bother to wipe the falling tears that's running down the side of his face he lifted his head up kissing her again while he lifted up her dress and slides his hands underneath it connecting with her soft skin as he twisted up his fingers around the sides of her lace thong ripping it off aggressively. Not thinking about messing up her hair she slid her dress over her head. His dick immediately becomes hard from the stiffness of her nipples that looked even better than how he last remembered them. The sexual urge that he been fighting to keep under control since he first saw her was now unleash taking over his body and soul he pulled her down on him after quickly slid his jeans and boxer off tossing them to the side of the bed pushing his tongue deep into her mouth, he feels her body shiver after letting out a loud moan. She spread her legs over his hips took in a deep breath and let it out as she is forced to slides down on his manhood. He grabbed a hold of both her breasts rubbing them together and then sucking them one at a time as well as all over her abdomen and at times leave traces of marks on her neck repeating the act until she was wet enough to take in every inch without much pain. She pushed down even harder so she could feel him deep inside her. She moved her body back and forth, up and down faster than she had ever imagined that she could. He takes one hand and spread the lips of her vagina and uses his thumb to make small circles on her clit.

*I'm not sure if it's the love for Troy or is the excitement of cheating on my husband, or it's the luck of sex that make me cum so hard but I'm sure my heart is going to jump out of chest.* She thought to her self.

"You like how it feel inna you sexy?" He asks in an erotic tone as he sits up and wraps his hand around her waist helping her to move faster. With her mind going crazy she couldn't get it to form an answer until moments later she said softly, "Yes baby it feel so good."

"Turn back way." He said, she hopped off and did as he asked with her feet hanging off the edge of the bed. He stood behind her and began rubbing the head of his hardness against her clit she screamed as he gives her the feelings that her body was destine for. He sinks deeper inside of her and listened to her as she begged him to cum with her this time and so he did. He fell on top of her and rolled over to the side and put his head on her chest trying to catch his breath until he fell asleep. Careen refused to go to sleep instead she made her mind wanders about what had happen. *I feel so sexy, so needed and beautiful this is how I dreamed my life would be, I have no idea how I ended up with Charles and stayed with him for so long Troy is the man I need to grow old with and the one that I want to experience my fairy tale marriage with, as my parents did but still I miss Charles a part of me wanted to go home and hold him tight cry on his shoulders and beg for his forgiveness and the next part hated him badly for the pain that he had cause me in a way that I thought wasn't possible but he's still my husband and his bed is where I should be.* She thought as she carefully lifted Troy head up and put it on one of his pillow she gets up and walks into the bathroom turning on the pipe running the water until it becomes warm the running of the water prevents her from hearing Troy's footsteps. "What are you doing"? He asks rubbing his eyes and yawning. I'm going to take a shower, I have to go."

"At two in the morning?" He asked sounding disappointed and confused. "I have to go Charles is home alone he must be worried, I will come by tomorrow I promise."

"No you're not going anywhere, you said Lacy was with her friend next door I'm sure she is good, and Charles don't care Careen, check your phone and see if him call you." She sits on the side of the tub and buried her face in the bath towel searching for a reason to leave and remembering that her friends once asks her to do the same and told her that Charles doesn't care about where in the world she might be. She now knew for sure that wherever he is he is not worrying about her so she wasn't going to waste her energy on him. She remembered what Mrs. Spencer had said, to find whom or what is it that makes her happy and stay with it. Troy is the only one that makes her happy and being with him is what makes her happy. "I don't have anything to sleep in she said." He gazes at her as if he was trying to see through her thoughts for a reason that makes sense. "You can wear one of my T-shirts there is no need for under wear because you won't be needing them. I knew it would be pointless arguing with him and the thought of sleeping in bed with the fabric from his T-shirt rubbing against my naked body and the tip of my uncovered nipples with no panties on is making me hot and putting me in the mood for another two hours of unbelievable wild sex.

Troy was awaken by the smell of fried dumpling and selfish that was coming from down stairs he rushed to the bathroom to wash his face and brush his teeth before he went down to see the face of the only woman in the world that made him feel like a boy again the one that made his stomach roll over every time she smiles. "Good morning handsome." She said as she put the cover on the pot and turned around in his arms. "Good morning to you darling." He said as she threw her hands around his neck. He used both of his hands and lifted up his T-shirt slowly over her hips and wasn't surprise that she still wasn't wearing any underwear. He immediately felt the heat rush through his body giving him an instant erection he scooped her up, putting her on the kitchen counter roughly but carefully spread her legs open with her still holding her tightly on to his neck, she bit her bottom lip and gaze into his eyes. "I need you so bad baby" she said in a passionate voice.

"I know you do Careen my body and soul belongs to you." He said while he forced his manhood deep inside her then bit on the nipples of her breasts, he ripped off the T-shirt exposing her naked flesh that pressed closely against his he picked her up pushing her back against the wall as she stood putting up one foot on his shoulder as he wined slowly pushing in deeper inside her forcing her to let out a moan. He carried her over the huge dining room table laid her on her back and asked her to spread her legs giving him the chance to use his tongue inside her. Once again he has fulfill her needs and she was completely relaxed after she had cum. He turn her around back way and slide his manhood inside her pulling it in and out until she begged him to fuck her harder, making himself cum before she was interrupted by the ringing of her phone. She gets up and ran over to the sofa grab her purse and began digging through it with the thought of Charles on her mind. "Hello."

"Careen I need you over here now!" Charles shouted from the other end of the line She hung up the phone and pulled on her jeans ignoring Troy who was still laying on the table catching his breathe. "Where you rushing off to Careen?" He asked the question that he is now tired of asking.

"Charles called me, I have to get home right now." He jumps off the table and ran over to her while his dick bounced from side to side. "You no have to go no where Careen, as this fool call you, you just going to run outta here like this? Not even thinking bout having some breakfast with mi." She was already dressed and making her way out with her keys in her hand "I'm sorry Troy this is why I didn't want us to make love because you now feel like sah mi a use you."

"Do what you have to do Careen, you're old enough and sure as well smart enough to know what you want and if Charles makes you happy and a him yuh want then gwan, just lose mi number and don't come back a mi yard." Without waiting for a response he slammed the door in her face and returned to the kitchen turned the stove off and went to his bathroom to have shower.

# Chapter 31
## Busted:

Careen flung the huge wooden door to her mansion open and walked straight toward the kitchen to get a glass of water and was frighten by the sight of Charles sitting at the table staring at the rising steam coming from his cup of tea.

"Charles, when you call me earlier why yuh didn't let me know you're home instead of having me drove all the way to your office?" She asks him while she makes your self a cup of tea and joins him around the table "Did I ask you to go to my office?" He sighs in frustration still refusing to acknowledge her presence.

"No Charles, but you called me on your cell phone and all the years that we had been together you had never taken a day off. So how would I know that you would be here, anyway why did you call me over here?" She stared into his eyes that looked as if he hadn't slept for days.

"I need my red shirt I've been looking for it and for some reason I cannot find it."

"Did you look in your closet?" She asked.

"No." his eyes now turned to her.

"Well it's hanging in your closet, you could've asked me

that over the phone instead of wasting my time. He ignored her comments and got up from the table dragging himself over to the sink turned on the pipe and began washing the cup. "You want to have lunch with me?" she asks taking a cautious sip of her hot tea.

" Careen because I'm home that doesn't mean that I don't have something to do are somewhere to go, now can you please leave me alone I have a lot on my mind and your voice is the last thing I want to hear right now." He said in a husky tone as he turned his attention back to washing the cup. Without saying a word Careen removed herself from the table and walked out to the verandah to gain the privacy of using her cell phone. She nervously dials Kerry-Ann home number hoping that she would be there.

"Hello, Kerry-Ann" She said calmly.

"Wah gwan Careen?"

" I need a favor if you are not busy today," as she looked behind her making sure that Charles wasn't close enough to over hear her conversation. "I need you to call Destiny and meet me over here in twenty minutes, drive Dwayne's car and pull up around the back of my house and wait for me there."

"Everything okay Careen?"

"Yes man mi good I'll explain it to you when you come just get Destiny."

"Okay see you inna few then." Kerry-Ann hung up and immediately speed dials Destiny's cell. "Who is this?" Destiny shouted from the other end as she fights to catch her breath. "What are you doing Destiny?"

"Mi dah pon luck down with Anthony wah you want?"

"Listen get dressed mi a come pick you up now Careen need us for reason that I don't know about yet."

"You fool Kerry-Ann? Mi just sah mi dah pon luck down that mean mi nuh left this yah dick fi now so gwan over Careen and let mi know later what happen" "Destiny mi a pick you up now so just get ready, you fuck too much."

"This is the fuckry mi a chat 'bout it cause too much to have friends." "Whatever just put some clothes on." without waiting for a response Destiny hung up the phone and threw it across the room. "Anthony I'm sorry baby Careen need me I have to go." She pushed him off her and headed to the bathroom.

"Why are we sitting in the car in your back yard Careen?" Destiny asked, "We are going to follow Charles it's time for me to close this chapter in my life and I cannot do that without me knowing what is his reason for the mistreatment that he had given me over the years and why his happiness only lasted the first year of our marriage."

"It's about time Sis", said Kerry-Ann, "well I guess this is worth me leaving a hard dick." Destiny said as she eased back in the back seat of the car and put on her sunglasses. Kerry-Ann looked over at her and rolled her eyes. "You need to cut out your childish ways Destiny all you care about is sex, food and sleep."

"I care about god, my daughter, my parents, but without sex, food and sleep how can I live and I need to live to continued to care about the people and things that mean the most to me so let's put it this way these things are like medicine that keep me going every day". She said with a huge smile on her face. Careen laughed out loud covering her face with her hand "Destiny you're a idiot she said as she looked at her. "Okay Careen there is Charles now" Kerry-Ann said.

"Start up the car!" They waited until he pulled out, then Kerry Ann slowly pulls out behind him they followed him for fifteen minutes until he pulls up at an unfamiliar restaurant. "Mi asks the pussy fi tek me fi lunch and him refuse, why would he choose to come eat by himself. Careen kisses her teeth and rolled her eyes in frustration.

"Wait a minute Careen why is pastor here?" Destiny asks out of curiosity. Careen immediately remembered what Mrs. Spencer had said about pastor she swung the car door open, quickly pushed her head out side and began to vomit over the thoughts of Charles and him. They watched the two of them finished up their meal a couple of minutes later pastor pulls out and then Charles behind him. "I've been driving for about half an hour now Careen, where are they going?" Ask Kerry Ann. they're going have sex, " shut up Destiny!" Kerry-Ann yells at her.

"Lord have mercy pon you, mi don't know why you can't behave like a human being."

"Why mi must pretty it up Kerry-Ann it's obvious that Charles is a batty man we just didn't know who didda fuck him or who him didda fuck now we know" "Don't jump to conclusion yet Destiny." said Kerry-Ann gazing over to see the reaction on Careen's face. "Don't listen to Destiny Careen she doesn't know any better she was curse from the day that she was born."

"Sah what you want Kerry-Ann." they pulled off the road behind him as he turned onto a small road; the road was just dirt and stone causing their car to move from side to side. They stopped and watched them pull up to a small board house. "Pull off the road Kerry-Ann stop behind these bushes." said Destiny. "Okay what now Careen?" They both asked if she needed pictures, "Yes, but I'm not going anywhere near that house. "I will take the pictures Kerry-Ann stay with her 'til mi come back" Destiny said as she reached over and took the camera from Careen hands. "Don't you shed any tears over him Careen?"

"These tears aren't for Charles Kerry-Ann but for me, for giving this man nine best years of my life. I loved and supported him; I always made him feel like a man even when he didn't act like one."

"I know sis, it must be hurting you like crazy but you give this fool nine years of your life not all your life Careen you can move on and I'm sure you will be happy once Charles is out of your life." Kerry-Ann gave her a hug and wiped her tears.

Destiny knocked on the car window to get their attention. "Open the door Careen." She said in an upset voice.

"What happened Destiny?"

" Careen I don't want to talk about it, all I have to sah is that Charles deserved fi get some gun-shot, clean the pictures and look at them fi you self I just need to get home and clear my head.

"Ok we will drop you home just calm down." Careen said, she slid into the back of the car closed the door and ask Kerry-Ann to drive the car.

# Chapter 32
## Your arms is all I need:

"Oh so you a break inna mi house now?" Troy opens his door to see Careen sitting steadily on his couch gazing at the trees that were moving from side to side from the heavy blowing of the summer breeze. "I didn't break in here Troy you gave me a key last night." He moved closer to face her, but she turned her face away as he sit down beside her. "I apologize I guess it slip my mind and mi also sorry fi what I said yesterday about you not coming back here I was angry."

"No need to say you're sorry I would had done the same if I was in your position." He hold her hand and started noticing her well manicure fingers and let it go when he felt his heart tighten from the sight of her ring. He eased back into the sofa and sighed. "What can I do for you Careen?"

"Nothing I just needed to get away from my house for awhile."

"Awhile as in you want to stay here?" He jumped up from the sofa in excitement then settle back down when he realized that she might changes her mind. "Yes Lacy and I need to stay here for awhile." "You and your daughter can stay here as long as you like baby" He broke into a smile. "Why can't

182

you face me Careen?" He walked around the other end of the sofa to see her face and tried to look in her eyes. She jumped up from her sitting position and walked over to the window, still refusing to look at him. He walked up behind her, even though his main focus is to find out what's her propose for shielding her face from him. He couldn't help but to admired her short dress that's fitted to her curves as if it made just for her. He ignored her struggles and swung her around only to gaze into the face that was once clear with not even a freckle is now black and blue with swollen eyes. He let her go without asking any questions are making any comments he ran toward the front door fighting to pull the keys from his pocket. "Troy wait, don't go over there." As she ran behind him yelling and crying, before he could get into his car she caught up to him. "Baby, please don't do this."

"Careen get off me look what the pussy done to you, him can't get away with this."

"I know baby, but on my way over here I stop at the police station and made a statement." He was still struggling to push her away so he could open the door. "I can't let you get in trouble for me, just please come sit inside with me and I'll tell you what happened." She slowly convinced him until he reluctantly gave in. They went inside and he helped her lay down on her back then he removed her sandals, he went back down stairs to fetch her a cold drink of water. He removed his jacket and shoes before he joined her and listened to what she had to say. "I was home getting ready to go pick up Lacy from her friends, when I heard Charles coming up the stairs I purposely ignore him until he grabs my wrist and pulls me toward him I wasn't sure what was on his mind, but I instantly become nervous. I had never seen him like that before. He ordered me to make him something to eat and I refused pulling away from his grip and continued getting dressed, he pushed me down on the bed and started punching me, I was so fucking scared and surprised he was hitting me with frustration as if he had no idea what he was doing, and he wasn't sure that it was me, not giving me a chance to fight back when he was satisfy and he got off me. It was then I knew that the fucker knew exactly what he was doing because he asked me again to go make him something to eat". Troy tightens his teeth fighting hard not to let his anger show he pulled her close and kissed her cheek. "I wait until he went into the bathroom and I wasted no time getting out of the house and drove away.

"Don't you ever try to find a reason to defend his abusive ways Careen he knew exactly what he was doing when he hit you and for a woman that's this strong and beautiful as you doesn't deserve that kind of treatment." His voice was strong with promises she knew that Troy was all she needed. He's strong, a fighter, a survivor and knows how to treat her he was all man and a good one as well, which is not easily find in these days. She glance down at her watch and jumped off the bed. "I have to go Troy."

"Where are you going now?"

"I have to go get Lacy she's probably worried."

"I'm coming with you." He walked around the bed to get his jacket.

"No baby, I'm just going to get some clothes for us to go with Destiny to St. Elizabeth this weekend and pick up my daughter just try and get some sleep until mi come back give me two to three hours. I promise I'll be back." She kissed his lips and walked out the room.

# Chapter 33
## I held her for the first time:

Two hours later Careen pulled up in the driveway of Troy's luxurious apartment she watched him run over with a warm and welcoming smile. "I was just about to come look fi you," he said opening the driver's door and helps her out. "Troy please, it's only been two hours since I left I asked you to get some sleep."

"How can I sleep when the only woman that makes my heart skip a beat is coming to stay at my home?

"Is this little Lacy? He pushes his head inside to look at her.

"Yes it is," she walks around to the passenger side to open Lucy's door. "Come on" Careen said taking the hand of her daughter helping her out. "Lacy this is the man that I was telling you about earlier."

"Ok mummy." She jumps out and ran into his arms. He immediately felt a connection to her that he never thought he would. Her face matches his that led him to gaze at Careen for an answer without him have to ask the question but instead she gazed back without saying a word. "Come on Lacy let me show you your room." he lifted her up and carried her bags leaving Careen standing there with hers. "This is your TV you can watch all the cartoons that you want."

"Thank you sir." She said with a shy smile.

"You can call me Troy for now, you are so polite and beautiful, just like your Mummy." he said sitting at the edge of the bed staring deep into her face comparing the color of her eyes the shape of her nose even her smile shows much resemblance as well, the curls in hair and the complexion of her skin. *This child has to be mine,* he said to himself, *but why would Careen hide it from me*? He had every intention of finding out the truth. "Lacy stay here I'm going to check on mummy."

"Yes Troy and thank you for the complement earlier."

"You're welcome sweetheart mi soon come back if you need anything just come down stairs."

"I will, but I should be fine" She said. He walked out pulled the door shut behind him after he holds her tight in his arms. "Careen!" he shouted at her from the living room making his way over to the dining room.

"Oh hi baby I'm just setting the table so we can have dinner." He decided to keep his question until another time when he remembered that the only thing that he had ever eaten at this table is between her thighs flashbacks of him laying her flat on her back entering her, pushing deep down inside her with every passion and love that he had ever felt for her gave him an instant hard-on. He walked toward her and hugged her from behind. "I'll bring the food to the table, just finish setting the table" He whispered close to her ear.

"Ok but just a little bit I don't eat like how I use to I have a child now and I have to watch this figure" turning around in his arms to look at his expression.

"In my eyes, you'll always be the sexiest woman in Jamaica" kissing her on her lips until she goes deeper getting a hold of his tongue and began caressing it with hers. After dinner Careen showered Lacy and got her ready for bed, she also read her a bedtime story until she fell asleep; she then went into Troy's room and closed the door half way. "I wanted to tell you for the longest time how beautiful you look in that nightgown," he said as he fluffed up her pillow and waited anxiously for her to join him. "Don't be extra nice Troy because you're not getting none tonight."

"You must be out of your mind, you can't come inna mi bed looking so sexy and no wah give up none" she laughs, and pulls the sheet half way down and slides under it, putting her head on his chest. "I have a question to ask you Careen and I need the truth, can you do that fi me"? He asks in a soft voice running his fingers through her hair inhaling the unfamiliar sweet scent of her shampoo. Her stomach tightens as her breath becomes difficult to catch. Her voice trembles as she asks, "what is it Troy?"

"Is Lacy my daughter? I just need to hear it from your mouth because I already figured out the answer."

"And how did you figure that much." She raises her head and lifts a brow to hear what was coming next. "She looks just like me, her hair has curls just like mine and her complexion is the same."

"She is your daughter." Tears began to fall down her cheeks. He lay there in silence for three minutes hoping his pain would ease before he allowed any words to leave his mouth. "Why did you do this to me Careen? All I had done and still doing is love you ever since the night I ask you to be my girl."

"I'm sorry baby, there is nothing that I can say to decrease your anger and numb the pain that you are feeling. But after I got involved with Charles I then focused on finishing my career and raising her in the best way I knew how, a year after I got married complications and worries started to come my way and I couldn't bothered searching for you anymore. I thought you had moved on and wanted nothing to do with me." She wiped the fallen tears from her face and eased back in his arms for comfort. "I missed nine years of her life, how am I going to be a good father now? What do I say?" He rubs his forehead and exhales.

"I explained everything to her before we got over here she already knows that you are her father."

"This shit even hurt more hearing the truth from your lips than when I was guessing it". He carefully pushes her off him so that he could get up.

"Listen Troy, if you want me to leave I will the last fucking nine years had been the hardest and the most challenging time of my life. I'm trying to change things around for my daughter and I."

"The choice was yours Careen, you chose to leave me and be with the first ass hole who might had said something good to you, something that he thought you would want to hear at that time." She was surprise by the loudness of his voice and the look of anger on his face she jumped off the bed and picked up her purse she got a hold of the pictures and threw them at him. "I didn't chose this but is what I ended up with for nine years, I did everything under the sun to make this man love me I prayed for our marriage more than how I prayed for my daughter, I did everything to make him happy and turn our house into a home, but all that I did, still drove him into pastor's bed. He looked at each picture in amazement as his anger turned to laughter causing him to roll off the bed. "Careen, you mean to tell mi sah you left mi fi a real battybwoy?" He laughed out loud again, "no man! All of these must burn with a word of prayer, my god!" He said still gazing at the pictures, "isn't pastor married?" He asked looking puzzled

"Yes Troy, when you feel like you've enough put dem back inna mi bag I'm going to sleep. I need some peace." He looked up and realized that she was hurting. He reached over for her purse and put the pictures in it just as she had asked and lay down beside her. "You ok, baby?"

"Yes I will be fine. I have the strength that god gave to us women to fight any tribulation that might come our way, and time heals." she said

"Time only heals what we want it to, sexy. But I'm here for you and will always be as long as you want me to. I will help you find happiness again." He leaned over and kissed her on her cheek. Before he could finish his next sentence she was fast asleep but he didn't care she was right where he had prayed for years for her to be in his bed laying in his arms with his daughter in the next room across the hall. He finally finds happiness and a reason to live again.

# Chapter 34
# Unwanted memories and feelings:

The sweet smell of fried fish and roasted breadfruit welcomed us as we pulled up in the driveway of the house I use to sometimes call home after mummy and daddy died. I now hate coming back here because my mind floods with memories that bring nothing but unbearable pain that makes me weak and sick for days. In every room of this house holds a picture of my parents in a hand carved frame that is dusted every day and night and put out in the community every holiday for people to pay their respects and say a word of prayer.

"Lord Jesus! Look at my babies." Destiny's mother ran toward them with open arms and a big smile with her husband behind her trying his best to keep up. "Hi Careen, you grow up so pretty, you look so nice Kingston agrees with you man I wish yuh mother was here to see yuh now."

"Thank you so much ma'am yuh look good yuh self, you 'haven't aged a bit."

"It might not show on my face, but it is surely affecting my bedroom performance." She laughs and looks over at her daughter Destiny who always has a comment for everything. "No body no wah hear bout that mummy."

"Stop yuh nose and give mi, mi granddaughter a who is this handsome young man you hold on to so tight like sah breeze a go take him from yuh."

"This is Anthony, my boyfriend."

"Nice to meet you young man she give him a small hug. Destiny is twenty seven and you is the first man mi ever meet, at one point mi believe sah she was one a dem thing dah wah sleep with other woman, wah dem call dem"? She looks at Careen for an answer but she was too busy laughing to respond. "They're call lesbians mother, and no I'm not one nor was I one." Destiny said while kissing her teeth and walks over to her father gives him a huge bear hug and a kiss on his cheek. "Hello daddy, it's good to see you again."

"Don't pay your mother no mind." He whispered in her ear that brought a smile to her face. After taking the time to get acquainted with each other over one of the biggest meals any of them had yet to have in years, Careen dropped Lacy off at her grandparents refusing to stay any longer than she had to. Destiny left Dasrine with her parents and Kerry-Ann dropped DJ off at her parents so he could spend some time with them and get to know them better.

"We had been driving for fifteen minutes now, how far up on this hill is the house Destiny?"

"Can you relax and enjoy the ride Kerry-Ann, if you did came up here with Careen and I last Summer you wouldn't have to ask," she said in a happy and calm voice. Two minutes later she parked in the driveway of her huge seven-bedroom mansion. She stepped out of her car feeling proud of what she had accomplished as she look around at the well cut lawn and the coconut trees blowing from side to side. "I guess selling yourself in Miami finally paid off, Kerry-Ann fights to get her words out through her laughter. "You always find a way fi disrespect me Kerry-Ann god give me ten fingers and two hands, a good brain, with my education and degree from the

University of the West Indies there is no reason to sell my self. And oh, here is a little lesson fi you." She dropped her bags and turned around to face her. "It's not how much money that you make that gives you big house and nice cars, but it's the amount of blessing that god rains upon you also the ambition and motivation that comes with it."

"Whatever Destiny," As she brushed passed her and headed toward the door making her way through the living room to find a bedroom."

"Hi, Miss Destiny" was a husky familiar voice that instantly took her back in time. She leans on her car trying her best to hold myself up from hitting the pavement face first from the sight of a boy that is now a man that makes her experience what it felt like to be with a real man and rocked her world in a way that no one had ever done before.

"Hi Handy," she said running in his open arms. *"God, I'm trying to be a good girl but I cannot do* it *by myself I need a hand"* she said to her self. He smelled even better than she had remembered the tightness of his big wide shoulders and the strength in his arms that wrapped tightly around her waist is taking her close to an orgasm as she close her legs and fight desperately not to wet herself, he let her go and eased back. *"Oh! Thank you god,"* she said to your self. "So what are you doing trespassing on my property?" she asks giving him a shy smile.

"I thought you gave me the permission he laughed and gazed into her face refusing eye contact. I'm sorry; your mother hired me to take care of your lawn," He said. She laughed, "I'm sorry I meant the lawn, I now own my own landscape company," he said looking down at the ground.

"That's good, I'm proud of you." She said removing the hair from her face. . "But I have to give yuh your props as well, a big mention pon top a the hill and one of Kingston finest gynecologist. "Thank you".

"You chose a good line of career you had always known how to use your tools."

"Oh god, I'm sorry Handy that didn't come out right." She said nervously

"Don't worry about it I know what you meant." He opened the passenger side of his truck on sat down staring at the polish designs on her toes and then wonders how she get her hair to style like that. "Why are you looking at me like that?" she asks cautiously not sure if she wanted to know why.

"Because I'm nervous," he answers her, sounding convincing. "Why are you nervous she steps closer to him?"

"Because I'm still in love with you." He jumps from his truck throws his arms around her pulling her closer to him he pushes his tongue into her mouth and she returns his kiss memories of the two of them making love races through her mind as she sinks deeper into his mouth, pushing her hands beneath his shirt caressing his rock hard stomach as her hand sinks down between each of his packs he grabs her breasts in his palms squeezing them together in the midst of unbuttoning his pants and him tearing his mouth from her neck to catch his breath she realizes what is going on she pushes him off. "I can't do this I'm sorry, Anthony is in love with me." She said sadly "But are you in love with him?" he asks as she pulls away her hands from his and ran inside closing the door behind her. Luckily Anthony was busy playing and betting on video games with Troy and Dwayne he didn't have a clue about what had happen. Kerry-Anne and Careen were in the kitchen arguing about what to cook for dinner. "Wah gwan sis, how you friend Handy change up so much, he look better than before, seems taller, his body is definitely appears to be firmer and him look fuckable."

"Kerry-Ann, I would never thought in a million years that those words would ever left your mouth about another man," Careen said.

"All of us women think about other men we just have to

know our place and don't act upon it, right Destiny?" She turned her attention to her standing at the entrance of the kitchen looking guilty. "Destiny you okay?"

"Yah man mi good." She walked over and pulled out a chair and slowly sits down. *There is no need for me to try and figure out what's my feelings toward Handy because god knows that he's the only man that I had ever loved, but stupid me because he wasn't accepted by everyone else. I hid my love and tried to forget about the feelings that I carried for him, but it is too late now there is no way that I'm going to are ever hurt Anthony.* Destiny thought to your self.

# Chapter 35
## The decision:

"I'm so tired," Careen said making her way to the bathroom to join Troy in the shower. After he was done giving her a bath and covered her body with lotion she sat down on the floor in front of him gazing at the stars in the beautiful night sky as he brushes and catches her hair up in a pony- tail. "This is so peaceful I wish our lives could be like this forever".

"Baby this can be one of your wishes that I can full fill if you give me the chance." He said while he tickles her neck with his warm lips causing her to laugh out loud. "I'm still going through a healing process and I need some more time at least to get my divorce final and move out completely." She said gaining back her seriousness. "I understand, but I just can't wait for the chance to make you happy, gives you more than you are worth and shower you with all that you deserve." She held him in her arms and embraces him with everything that she ever felt for him.

Saturday arrived but they were all disappointed their plans for spending the day at the river wasn't going to happen, it was pouring rain and dark outside since the night before. Careen and Kerry-Ann decided to make breakfast. "Did you hear Destiny and Anthony fucking last night?" Kerry-Ann laughs at the question that Careen had just asked. "Yes I did, didn't you hear me yelling at them to cut it out other people is in the house, but instead Destiny decided to moan and scream even louder." "Morning Kerry-Ann, Careen." Destiny said as they watched her walks over to the fridge rubbing her eyes and grinning in excitement. "Mornin ladies, what's up Troy, Dwayne," Anthony said as he made his way into the kitchen behind her. They wanted badly to discuss what had happen but they hate to discuss their sex lives in front of their man so they left it for one of their girl's day out.

"Dwayne I need to have a word with you please." Kerry-Ann said taking the lead toward the dining room.

"Yes, Kerry-Ann." why in the middle of sex last night you got up and ran to the bathroom bringing up everything that could came up, are you sick"?

"Mi no know, maybe mi have a stomach virus or something, mi use to only vomit inna the morning time but now it a get worst." He said while he rubs his stomach and gazed in her eyes for a word of healing. "When did you start feeling like this? She asks looking curious.

"Two weeks I didn't said anything 'cause I didn't want to worry you about something as simple as a stomach virus." She turned her attention to the window as she glance down at her stomach and then walked over to the calendar and checked the dates remembering that her period is four weeks late. "Dwayne Gwan back up stairs go lay down mi soon come talk to you" without responding he turns around and ran up the stairs.

He had almost fallen asleep when he saw a shadow from beneath the door moving closer toward it, he propped up his head on the pillow in a sitting position and watched as the door knob turned to the right and pushed open he was surprise by who came in and closed the door tightly behind her. "Wah you want, didn't you get enough fuck last night? He ask looking angry and disappointed that it wasn't Kerry-Ann. "Don't be disrespectful Dwayne we might not be fucking anymore but I'm still the mother of your daughter." He kisses his teeth and covered his face with one of the pillow. "You didn't answer my question yet" his words struggle from beneath the pillow.

"Mi need fi talk to you and yes mi got enough sex last time" she leaned her ass against the edge of the dresser staring at him acting like a toddler with the pillow over his face she walk over and dragged it away from him. "How can I talk to you when your mind is somewhere else."

"Mi belly a hurt mi, mi feel sick and the last thing wah mi need right now is your talking."

"Well it's not me this time" she take two steps back" "wah yuh a chat bout?" He swings his feet off the bed and sits up, waiting patiently for her to finish. "You felt the same way when I told you I was pregnant, right?" She waits for his answer.

"Yes"

"Then your wife to be is pregnant" " why she's hiding it?" He asks with a clueless look covering his face.

"Maybe she don't know yet are not sure, anyway I'm here for something else, I'm going to tell Kerry-Ann about our secret affair". He jumped over the bed and ran toward the door to make sure that no one especially Kerry-Ann wasn't anywhere near by to over hear her. He turns and looks over at her standing in the corner of the room. "You must be out of your damn mind?" he realized that he was too loud and toned his voice down to almost silent. "Do you know what the fuck this will do to our relationship, I love Kerry-Ann there is no way mi a go put her through so much pain."

"Anthony ask me to marry him last night, Dwayne mi can't move on with this burden pon mi shoulder, I'm hurting here too and I believe that we all would feel better if we get this out in the open."

"You really pushing fi mek she put mi outside fi sleep with the dogs right?" he asks in a sad voice.

"You need fi man up about this and take responsibility for your actions."

"My fucking actions Destiny," he realizes that he was yelling again. "Remember sah yuh still continue to fuck mi even after you found out sah she a yuh friend so don't blame this all on mi."

"That's why I have to tell her she is my friend and I did her wrong so I will woman up to it and if I have to lose a her friendship for that then I guess the saying is true that nothing lasts forever". He sees that her mind is made up and nothing that he says will ever change it.

"When are you going to tell her?" He asks.

"Today." she said while making her way out.

"Hold on a minute." He walked over to her "I would come with you but mi just can't see she a cry and I want you to know that I wish you nothing but happiness with Anthony" for the first time their hug was sincere filled with nothing but love from one friend to another.

# Chapter 36
## Drama and excitement:

Destiny walked down the stairs counting each of the steps in her mind listening to the beating rain against the huge glass windows. She was trying to figure out the best way to approach her friend with the most painful news that she is yet to hear. She walked slowly throughout the house looking for her. She tried calling out for her but her lips felt heavy as her heart pounded from nervousness. She glanced her sitting on the verandah with her feet up on the other chair leaning her head to one side looking sad. "You ok Kerry-Ann"

"Yes."

"Why are you not up stairs with Dwayne?" she hesitates "No reason". Destiny picked up that something wasn't right she had never seen her act like this before her answer and questions always followed by a comment, reason and suggestion. Her womanly instinct tells her that this isn't the right time to inform her that she was sleeping with her man so she walked away and sits in the living room and switches on the television and began watching some music videos. Careen finally unwrapped her self from Troy's arms and asked Kerry-Ann to help her with dinner she realize that something was wrong when she saw the look of worry on her face, but didn't bother to ask why. She followed her with her eyes as she watched her get up from the verandah and brushed past her and went into the guest bed- room slamming the door behind her. Without knocking she pushed the door open and lay on the bed besides her staring directly in her face. "Wah gwan with you sis and don't tell mi nothing cause mi never seen you like this before. It hurts to see the tears fall from your eyes for reasons that I'm still waiting on." Careen said while she wipes the tears from her friend eye.

"You remember when I told you that I believe Dwayne is cheating on me?"

"Yes" Careen answer looking confuse and scared not wanting to know what she is about to say next " and that I had no idea who the girl is?" Kerry-Ann asks again.

"Yes." She nodded her head hoping that she would just tell her and stop with the questions. "Well I lied," as she sobs and wiped her face. "So you know the girl?" Careen asks.

"Yes."

"Who the fuck is she?" Kerry-Ann remains in silence.

"Answer mi no, a who the bitch?"

"Destiny" she cried even more soon as the familiar name left her lips.

"You want mi fi get Destiny."

"No Careen, Dwayne and Destiny been fucking around behind mi back for how long I don't know but mi just see her go up stairs to him". Kerry-Ann said out loud. Careen fell to the floor and covered her mouth from not letting her scream make it way to down stairs. She gets up and runs toward the door forcefully pulling it open Kerry-Ann gets up and run behind her holding on to her elbow restraining her from finding Destiny. "Please don't go down there I can't handle this right now I'm pregnant." She yells out.

"You what?"

"I'm pregnant." she repeated it twice hoping that it would change her mind.

"This is exactly why we need to confront her you need an explanation and a reason for this fuckry that the two of dem keep up." Careen pulled her arm away and ran down the steps. Troy you see Destiny?" Him and Anthony were busy drinking Heineken and playing cards he didn't hear her question. "Yuh see Destiny?" she shout causing him to jump spilling his drink on him self.

"She out dah so." Troy said while he cleans off his pants. Instead of walking around the table she jumped over it and walked up behind her. "Please tell mi sah it's not true sah you and Dwayne a fuck." Destiny looked up and see the tears in both of her friends eyes as well as the deadly look on both of them faces she remained seated and held her head down. "Yes it's true we were having an affair, but it ended nine years ago."

"Don't try to pretty it up - it's fucking- the only word for it." Careen shouted at her. Kerry-Ann sits on the handle of the chair and asks her why in a sad and soft voice. Destiny tells them both how Dwayne and her met, what happen then and what happen after, she even go as far as telling them that he is Dasrine father. Troy and Anthony already made there outside refusing to hear what they were talking about. Kerry-Ann didn't know what to say but to let her pain out through her tears Careen throws her arms around her hugging her tightly. "I need you to call everyone since we're all close enough to fuck each other I'm sure as hell that we can all sit down and talk about this, and I defiantly need to hear what Dwayne have to say." After hours of talking there was a lot of questions some answered and the remainders not even Dwayne or Destiny have on answer for. "My heart haven't drifted away from you Dwayne, god knows that I still love you and there is no point walking away from a good man over something that ended nine years ago, if it wasn't one of my best friends It wouldn't worth any tears but I cannot help but think of why you continued to have sex with her even when you found out that we're friends, someone that is so close to me, someone that I grew up with she's like my sister and it hurts. She subs while her lips trembled making it difficult for her to continued. "I don't know how long it will take for me to get over this maybe I never will, she sobs and wipes her face between her words. "Ever since we met, since I was a little girl everything about you has lighten my soul you filled my life with nothing but love and happiness. I will not abandon you for a reason that is bearable, what the both of you had shared was just a fuck and that I can live with, I forgive you." She looked over at him standing at the nearest exit using the tail of his shirt and wipes his tears. "Don't you ever take my forgiveness and tolerance for weakness, weeks from now I will walk down the aisle with my father and with every strength in my body I will stand in front of you and I say I do with every beat of my heart and then walk back down the aisle with you and stand by your side as your wife, like a woman should to a real man."

He walked over to her and fell down on his knees.

"Thank you Kerry-Ann, I'm so sorry and I promise that I will never hurt you again she wrapped her arms around him and gazed over at Destiny her face was red and her eyes swollen from crying for so long. "I forgive you Destiny, I will continue being your friend but as I said to Dwayne I need some time. "I love you Kerry-Ann and I'm sorry, really sorry."

"It's okay sis just don't mek it happen again she smiled at her.

Sunday morning:

I rolled over and looked into the face of the man that's laying next me and began to wonder why do I still love him so much, but when I look at the picture sits perfectly in the frame on the bedside table and the beautiful face that stars back at me I now know that I will do anything to make my son happy and breaking up with his father will break his heart and when I think about the way he makes me feel the way he touches me so tender, treats and give me all the respect that I deserve I would also be heartbroken even though he hurt me tremendously there is one thing I'm sure about and that is I'm still madly in love with him and with that I'll one day learn to put it behind me . "Kerry-Ann you okay?"

"Yes baby I'm good but I have something to tell you." He jumps up. "I'm pregnant I took the home pregnancy test this morning, I'm guessing I'm four weeks but I will know for sure Tuesday when I go to my appointment". He leans over and kiss her with nothing but laugher on his face. "It's a girl this time," he said sounding excited.

"I'm not arguing with you this time because last time you where right". She removes her lips from him and gets up. "Where are you going?"

"Down to the kitchen I'm going to make something to eat" She said.

"Mek mi go" He said.

"No baby I need to have a talk with my friends just stay up here mi soon come back" with that said he let her go. She looked out the window only to see Destiny and Anthony out there drinking coconut water chatting and laughing only added salt to her wound she gets angry and decided to let her know exactly how she feels. "You're a fucking bitch she yells as she walks closer to her."

"Don't call mi out of mi name Kerry-Ann I thought we been through this shit yesterday". She stands up looking puzzled by what could have caused her reaction. "No, you been through it I have to live with this fi the rest of mi life, you sleep with mi man and get up this morning acting as if everything should be okay, you put a dent in my relationship that is not fixable Destiny how could you do this to me?" she ask in a said voice. Not waiting for an answer she bent over and picked up a rock using it to hit her several times across her face.

"Jesus Christ," Anthony said, rushing to her side looking shocked." Kerry-Ann are you crazy?" he yells causing everyone to come running outside to see what was going on. "What happen to her? Careen turns and asked Kerry-Ann who was passing her in on haste.

"Don't ask mi no question." as she turns around and walks back inside. "She needs to go to the hospital she might need stitches." Careen said to Anthony. "You have to stitch her up Kerry-Ann you always walk with your medical kit." Troy said to her but she refused to remove her gaze from the orange that she's peeling. "Did you hear mi?" he asks heavily.

"Yes I did but what she needs is a gynecologist fi stitch up her pussy -hole so she can't fuck another woman's man."

"Fine Kerry-Ann since you're refusing to help her, we have to take her to the hospital. She watched him ran back out to help them put her in the car. As she gazed out the window and instantly felt sorry for her. "Bring her inside the living room" she yells at them. "Careen go and get my medical equipment, hurry up please." She put her head in her lap and immediately begins to clean the blood from her face she stitched her wound up in no time. She gazed into her face knowing that there is something that is has to say but couldn't find the words or the courage to apologize.

# Chapter 37
## How it all ends:

Sitting here in my driveway staring at the biggest house in Kingston as I look in the rear view mirror I can actually see the words printed on my forehead the saying is true that material things don't make anyone happy. Because all I can think about is Troy and the way he made me fell over the weekend it's the happiest I ever felt within the past nine years. With all the strength that I have I pull myself from around the steering wheel and walk slowly to my front door as I open it the one person I hope not to see is sitting at the table with his gun spinning around in circle.

"I should had stayed with Lacey and Troy, I don't know why the hell I come home to a house that only remembered my tears and the fights between my husband and I," she said to her self as she joined him around the kitchen table. "Where were you over the weekend"? With his eyes still glued to his gun he asked in a soft voice. She sighs and eased back in the chair. "I was in St. Elizabeth with Destiny and Kerry-Ann".

"Only with your two bitchy friends?" he asks looking over at me?

"No, we where accompany by our lovers and the fathers of our children, he lift a brow and take a deep breath as he adjusted himself to a comfortable position in the chair. "So who is this lover of yours Mrs. Anderson." she didn't felt that Troy deserve to be kept as a secret any more she is in love with him and could cared less about who gets hurt by it. "The name is Careen and I should corrected you not only is he my lover, but my best friend, my fiancé, my future husband, the father of my daughter and the only man that my heart ever beats for. "So you had yourself a nice little vocation, right?" He asks for the first time in their conversation he purposely caught her eyes. "Yes I did and the sex was great before she finishes in the blink of an eye he rushed over and grabs her by her neck pulling her up from off the chair slamming her back against the wall, pointing the gun in her face she hold on to his hands as she struggles to get her words out. "You're choking me" he let her go and slap her across her face without showing any care he watched her stumble and fall over the chairs. "No wonder why I couldn't get turn- on by your nasty rass because you out fucking the whole of Kingston." She slowly crawled over to her purse and pulled out the pictures throwing them across the floor, "This is the reason why you couldn't get turn-on by me Charles because you a batty-man your cock only can stand up by the sight of pastor and other men ass holes. His anger grows as he looks at each picture, "You turn investigator over night you fucking whore!" He yells while kicking her repeatedly in her stomach. "No, Charles please I'm pregnant the words sounded frazzle through the sound of her crying. He bent down over her. "What did you say, bitch?" He whispered. She subbed and exhaled, "I'm pregnant." She looked at him showing no sign of fear she manage to sit up and lean against the table and spit the blood from her mouth in his face. He wipes his face with his shirt and hit her across her face again. "What the fuck do I care, it wasn't my sperm that created what you carry in your womb so I can do what the fuck I want to you and it". He stood up and stares at her twisting from side to side in pain. "I will not fist fight with you Charles because I need this baby that I'm carrying and with you holding a gun in your hand feeling as if you are the world strongest man I'm pretty sure that you will do everything to keep that feeling if it means taking my life because it's the only thing that you got going for you now. Now I know why yuh family dem don't want to have anything to do with you and the only reason why you have friends is because of what you can do for them, you have money, and a woman as fine as myself in your house as your wife. But it will change after I put these up all over the Internet tomorrow she said while she tried to stand up holding her stomach in pain. "You might not live to see tomorrow Careen" he said giving her room to get up, without him noticing or give him time to react she pushed him over the table and ran up stairs locking herself inside their bedroom. "Open the door Careen!"

"No Charles she yells from behind the door she jumps over the bed picked up the phone and quickly dials 119. "Yes, this is Careen Anderson I was there almost a week ago can you send detective Brown over to my house my husband is trying to kill me".

"Where are you now ma'am."

"I'm locked in my bed room."

"Stay there I'll send him over right away."

"Thank you so much." She hangs up and picked it up again dialing the number to Troy's cell phone but hangs it up after the first ring. I cannot get him into this, I enter this relationship alone and alone I will exit it. The pounding on the door makes her heart race as she looks around for something to protect herself, she screams out from the sound of his gun that he fired twice to unlock the door, he walked over to her and pushed her into a laying position on the bed as he climbed on top of her. "You will stay fucking married to me, we will kiss and makeup and you will continue to be the wife that I trained you to be."

"You have a sick mind Charles you need help." She tried to push him off but he pinned her two hands down during their struggle his gun fell to the floor, he began hitting her across her face again taking pleasure in watching the blood splatter on the wall until he feels something tap him on his shoulder he stops and turns around to meet his gun pointed in his face. "Mi a beg pussy-hole please hit her again, just one more time hit her again."

"Who are you?" he said through his trembling voice.

"You no get fi ask mi no question, mi get fi tell you what the fuck to do and a only one question mi have fi you, you love beat woman?" He asked in a rough voice. "Answer mi battybwoy." He moved the gun up closer to his face.

"No." He said as his tears fell on Careen's bloody nose.

"The first thing mi want you fi do is fi yuh to get off mi rass woman, 'bout you hold her down a fist her inna her face." The hurt shows in his face as he kicks him off her and watches him fall to the carpeted floor and blood runs from the corner of his mouth. "Careen, baby you okay? He gazed over at her his hands started to shake when he didn't get any response right away and relaxed when she said, "Yes baby, I'm good."

"So a you a the bwoy that she's in love with." Charles ask holding his two hands up in the air he stares deadly into his eyes and pulls the trigger of the gun shooting him in his shoulder. "Mi sah you no get fi ask mi no question." Ignoring him pressing hard on the wounded spot he extended his hand out to help her sit up. "Give me the gun Troy." She looked into his eyes without saying anything or asking why he handed it slowly to her and watched as she walked over and kneeled down in front of him. "You remember when mi tell yuh sah I will not fist fight with you Charles?" He looks at her puzzled.

"Yes I remember." He started crying again. "Well, it wasn't because I was being weak or that I was afraid of you it was because I was being smart I know I would get my revenge so why fight with you then when I knew that you were unbeatable at that point?" She sighed and looked at him, "In all my life I play the role of being a good girl but what people don't know is that in every good girl there is a deadly and evil side to us we are like one of the deadliest snack strikes when no one has a clue we're coming and when we do we go after our prey with the intent to kill - tonight Charles you unleash the deadly and evil side of me." She wiped the blood from her face and with a look that her husband nor Troy had ever seen before she stood up walked back over to Troy and from the same distance that Troy was when he shots him she stands and pulls the trigger shooting him twice in his heart. When she took the gun from Troy she cleans it thoroughly with her dress to remove his fingerprint she turns to him and ask him to leave. "What are you talking about, I have to take you to the hospital" he said.

"The police are on their way." She looked out her bedroom window and watched them as they tried to break her door down. "You have to go now Troy if they find you here they will have no choice but to take you down for questioning and I cannot have you locked up for this, go through the back door!" She yells at him.

"Okay baby I love you."

"I love you too."

She lay down on the floor and pretended to be half dead as the police step over Charles lifeless body and ran over to her.

"Are you okay Mrs. Anderson she barley said "No" and as she hoped after the investigation the case was close in self defense.

"Troy thanks for coming over." She smiles at him sitting in the chair next to her bed holding her hand.

"You're well-come baby. I dropped Lacey off at Anthony house when you dial mi number and hang up I knew right then something was wrong. He kissed her on her swollen lips. "I'm pregnant with your child again."

"You truly made me the happiest man alive Careen." His eyes fill with tears, I love you so much. I will be a good father and a good husband I promise you." As he gets up to kiss her again he was interrupted by Destiny.

"All inna the hospital dem a mek love." She walks over and hug her friend with Kerry-Ann falling on both of them hugging and kissing each other in excitement.

"We love you Careen."

"I love you guys too." She looked at Troy and whispered, "I love you"

"I love you too." He whispered back.

# Acknowledgment

It feels so unreal laying on my belly on my bed with my son on my back typing the acknowledgement for a book that I wrote, but not surprising because I don't believe that there's anything I want and set my mind to that I don't get. This is the part where I thank everyone that is important to me and who might have helped me get this done so I will get straight to the point. First I would like to thank God not only for creating me, but for also granting me with the knowledge, the wisdom and courage to do this. Rarely people do this but I guess it's what makes me unique no one ever thanks them selves, but I'm going to go ahead and do it. I want to thank me for being self-motivated, for being strong and to believe that I could do this even if I didn't have the support of anyone. I want to thank my wonderful sister Lydia for helping with some of my editing work I love you girl stay strong. Thanks to my mother who is always there for me and never judges whatever decision I chooses in life, for always being proud of me and to her I'm the greatest if no one else will ever read this I know that she will. To my sister Alexa, brother Steven and Ashwani I love you three more than you will ever know. Thanks to Kenroy

Williams and Jason Logan for just being a talk away and to Clive James for being a friend. To Carlington S. for being a very special friend thank you for believing in me, whenever I felt like giving up I could always give you a call and you would heal whatever it is that I'm going through with your words. To Mershol Peat you are a blessing from god an angel that was send to be in the time that I needed one the most. Thank you for your continuous encouragement and the constant reminder of how talented I am when days of worries, tiredness and frustration had blinded my eyes for me to see it for myself. To my wonderful baby daddy Christopher I wonder sometimes how the hell you put up with my craziness for all these years I want to thank you for keeping our son from me when I needed time to work on this even when you didn't had a clue of what I was doing. To my grandmother Theresa, my Grandfather and my two Aunts thank you guys for raising me into the woman that I am today there is nothing that I can give or do that will ever match up to what you had done for me. To my Daddy for being the best father in the world and my Stepfather for being a part of my life, to all my cousins back home I love you guys. To my only friends Shadeen Gray, Tacine Lawson, Queen-Ann and Yanique Harris thank you all for being a part of my life. To my joy and my inspiration my son CJ you had brought out the best in me since the day that you were born, I felt the need and the reason to continue to fight to get to the top and with you in my life I have to continue climbing until I get there. I love you.

# Biography

Tracy-Ann Lewis was born on October 24, 1985 in the parish of Westmoreland Jamaica, to parents Dennis Lewis and Merverlyn Barrett. She was raise by her father Dennis Lewis, Grandmother Theresa Turner and her two aunts. They have nurtured, cared and protected her during the absent times of her mother. She moved to join her mother in the U.S in 1999 where she attended Weaver high school and graduated in 2003.

Tracy-Ann is now living in Connecticut with her fiancé of nine years and their two year- old sons and is enjoying the life of being a first time mom. She will continue to entertain Jamaicans with her writing and others that might find it interesting.

# About the book:

Careen move to Kingston to attend college at the University of the West Indies after the tragic death of her parents. Only to leave the one person that she had ever love behind and got married to her school counselor, who later with the help of Careen owned some of the best car dealers in Kingston. Everything wasn't all -good after she found out that he is gay and married to her only to prove to his friends and the community that he is not gay. Which lead him to beat her and refuse to have sex with her. Her two best friend Destiny and Kerry-Ann have all been friends since basic school all hell breaks loose when Destiny met the love of Kerry-Ann's life in Miami on one of her vacations and still continues the relationship with him even after she finds out that he was her friends boyfriend. Destiny finally breaks off the relationship when she was six months pregnant in college. She was still determine to tell Kerry-Ann about Dwayne and her sleeping around, before she get married to a man that she met on-line and ending up falling in love with him or so she thought, until she went back to the country for a vacation and reunited with the boy that she once had

214

sex with during the time of she sleeping with Kerry-Ann's boyfriend, all the feelings that she tries to hide and ignore has been rooted up again.

# A Word From The Author

*Don't always live for today are just in the moment. Even though it's sometimes true that we're only guaranteed today and this moment but always keep in mind that there's a possibility for tomorrow.*